Fake Dating the WINGER

Fake Dating
the WINGER
A TYRANTS HOCKEY NOVEL
JOSIE BLAKE

Content edits provided by Jessica Ruddick.

Cover photography by Wander Aguiar

Line editing suggestions provided by Red Adept Editing.

ISBN: 978-1-955887-15-1

Contents

Everyone needs a caretaker sometimes, even me. Thank you to George and my boys for being mine.

I love you all most.

Violet

"McCarthy must be on the rag. She was extra bitchy today." Lyle lifts his pint of craft beer. "Cheers."

"Fuck you, Lyle. If she was a man, you'd admire her leadership skills." Olivia shakes her head, taking a sip of her martini—extra dirty—without toasting with him. "She's feeling the crunch of this deadline too. I'm surprised she held it together as well as she did."

Secretly, I agree with them both. Our boss, Caitlyn McCarthy, was particularly short-tempered today. But I also think she manages our deadline fiascos better than anyone else could. Currently, she has to supervise our team during our client's software implementation. Meanwhile, senior management breathes down her neck nonstop. I feel bad for her, and I almost invited her out for drinks with us. She could probably use one. Or ten.

When the higher-ups assigned our team to this project, they said it was a mess. But the five of us are recent graduates, all desperate to get ahead at Kellerman's Consulting. When you're a newbie, you take the crappy assignments and say thank you.

The higher-ups weren't lying. The work has been grueling.

"There's no way we finish this project by Wednesday." Jonathan, another analyst on our team, sips his drink. "Their developers are the worst."

"Sepana is great," I chime in because I need to stick up for my girl. "She knows what she's talking about." Sepana is at PLG's headquarters in London. I met her last month when I traveled there for the project kickoff. My first impression was she was a problem solver, and she's proven it repeatedly since then.

"Doesn't hurt that you could probably program as well as she can if you wanted to." Lyle offers me a lazy grin that's probably half-sincere and half-flirtatious. The guy has been trying to get into my pants for over a month.

He's right, though. I have degrees in computer science and finance, but when I signed on for this job, the hiring manager insisted I wasn't to get involved in software development. Kellerman contracted us as financial analysts, and they didn't want us mucking around in code. But it's easier for me and Sepana to get things done when we're working in sync.

This isn't the crowd to say that in, though. I'm already a management favorite. It would sound like bragging, and I need to keep professional decorum.

So I change the subject. "Anyone going in the office tomorrow?"

The other four groan. But like me, they'll probably be there. It doesn't matter if it's a Saturday.

This time, when I hold up my drink—an old-fashioned, the way my daddy always made them—they join me. "To only one more week of PLG."

They all murmur their agreement, and the server arrives with the appetizers we ordered. The office ordered sandwiches for dinner, but they were nasty, and that was hours ago. *The glamorous life of a young professional.*

"What time is it?" I ask Olivia. My phone died before we left the office.

"Almost eight," she says, snagging a few nachos covered in pulled pork.

I reach for a plate. "Hunt said he might drop by tonight. I told him we might come here after work for drinks."

Lyle and Jonathan groan as they dig in, but Olivia perks up. "What time?" she asks, scanning the crowd. She wipes her hands on her napkin and smooths her hair. "Why didn't you say something sooner?" She glares at me. "Is he coming by himself?"

I only shrug. I didn't say anything because I knew she would act like this—all weird. Hunter Mason and I have known each other for years now, and we're good friends. Sometimes, I forget that he's a professional hockey player for the Philadelphia Tyrants. Apparently, Olivia doesn't forget. She has her compact out and is checking her makeup.

"He might just go home." It's always a toss-up with Hunt. Left to his own devices, he would probably stay home and read, or watch SportsCenter on repeat.

"Seriously, Vi. What's going on between you guys?" Lyle sets his drink down again. He winks at me as he picks up a fry. "Do I even have a chance?"

I laugh at him. "No. But not because of Hunter. We are coworkers." *Or as my daddy would say, don't shit where you eat.* I doubt Lyle would appreciate that Texas wisdom. "And Hunter and I are best friends." What I don't add is that his friendship is more important to me than anything.

"Well, if you don't plan to partake, I'm going to take a chance at him." Olivia snaps her compact closed and smiles. "He's delicious."

Though I keep my face expressionless, inside, I balk, and not only because Olivia used the word *delicious* to describe Hunter. Though seriously, who does that? I hate it when my friends talk about him like he's just some hot guy.

Since everyone's staring at me, waiting for me to respond, I shrug again. "Shoot your shot," I tell her, even though the words taste funny in my mouth.

Jonathan nudges his head toward the door. "You'll get your shot, Liv."

I follow his gaze to the entrance. Hunter's outlined in the door, his head almost reaching the top of the frame. Next to me, Olivia sighs. I barely stop myself from glaring at her.

But she's not wrong. Hunter Mason is something else. For one, he's in perfect physical condition. He has to be. He's a professional hockey player. This is his first year with the Tyrants, but they signed him during training camp, an uncommon occurrence. He works his ass off—always has. That probably explains how he moved from the third line to the second already. He's considered one of the top rookie forwards right now.

His body is amazing—he's tall, with wide shoulders and slim hips. He has shaggy brown hair and a dimple when he smiles. He wears glasses when he isn't on the ice, but he makes them look great in a nerdy way. Objectively, Olivia is right—he really is mouthwatering.

Not that I notice. He's my friend. We went to Chesterboro University together. The rest of our friends got scattered across the country since most of them are hockey players or dating hockey players. But we ended up in Philadelphia together. In the past six months, we have become even closer.

I doubt my coworkers are the only ones who have wondered if we're more than friends. But I'm not looking for a relationship. While Hunter's as hot as sin, I only do casual, and Hunter isn't a casual guy.

"I should go say hello and see if they want to join us." Standing, I use my napkin to wipe my fingers as Rocco Barnett and Colt Carmichael step inside behind Hunter. I smile. "Liv, Rocco and Colt are here too."

She grins, doing a silent fist pump. The guys groan, mumbling about how they'll get no game now, but I think it's mostly for show. It's impossible not to like Rocco and Colt. They're fun. As for Liv, she thinks they're almost as hot as Hunter. Not that it matters to me, though. Colt's my friend Shea's brother, so he's off-limits. Maybe under other circumstances, Rocco and I might have enjoyed some quality horizontal time together. If he weren't Hunter's teammate. For that reason alone, he's a no-go. It would be weird to see him afterward. I keep my sexual extracurriculars brief. Like one night. It's a rare occurrence when I want a repeat performance. I prefer to not even take a chance that things might get awkward. Not worth the effort.

"I'll go let them know where we're sitting." The words die in my mouth, though, because a ghost steps out from behind Rocco.

Nate Graham. My ex.

"Fuck," I whisper, though it's so quiet my colleagues probably don't hear me over the music in the lounge. Spinning on my stilettos, I avert my face from them all and suck in a deep breath. It doesn't smell great in this crowded bar, but whatever. Oxygen is oxygen.

I close my eyes and let my emotions wash over me—anger, hurt, and a lot of embarrassment. Nate and I dated my junior year at

Chesterboro when he was a senior and the starting goalie there. I was stupid in love with him. He signed with Denver, and I knew he would be on the other side of the country during my senior year. Naively, I figured we would make it work—that we were in it for the long haul.

Imagine my surprise when he headed off for training camp with a proverbial pat on the head and an "It's been fun."

Whatever. I learned a lot from that experience. That doesn't mean I want to see him, though.

Squaring my shoulders, I nod at my friends. "I'll be right back."

Lyle catches my arm. "You okay?"

That anyone noticed how I felt bothers me. I paste on my brightest smile, the one I used in pageants when I was a girl. "Absolutely. Just see an old friend."

My daddy always says that in business, you shouldn't let them see you sweat. Well, that's true in love and war, too.

Hunter

Please let Violet not be here.

Even as I think it, I don't mean it. I always want to see her. I just don't want her to be blindsided by Nate.

Not that I haven't been trying to get a hold of her for the past two hours. I've sent her repeated messages. As soon as Duke pulled me aside and told me the Tyrants signed my old teammate, Nate Graham, to take over for our injured goalie, Huck, I started spamming her: *Don't go out tonight. Call me.*

Of course, Duke would ask me to take Nate under my wing and show him around. He's right—Nate and I used to be close. Then things got complicated. Like, I-started-lusting-after-his-girlfriend kind of complicated.

As we step through the door to Pearl in the Sky, a bar in downtown Philadelphia, I check my phone again. All the messages I sent Violet are still unread. Clicking the screen black, I shake my head. Sometimes, I wonder why she has the phone since she lets it die so often.

The Pearl is crowded as usual. I do my best to keep the distaste off my face. This isn't my scene. The packed bar with its music so loud people need to yell to be heard over it... this is Violet's happy place. Colt and Rocco are cool with it too. Maybe they're all fine with it because they all grew up in urban places. Me? I'm from a farm in Missouri. All these people make me claustrophobic.

Behind me, Rocco whistles under his breath. "Is that a bachelorette party? I'll find you stiffs later." He slides off with more swagger than any person should have.

I barely acknowledge him as I scan the place for a tall, gorgeous blonde.

"This is a good place," Nate says from next to me. "Cool vibe."

Please don't be here...

But even as I think it, I see the top of her head coming toward us. My wish was futile anyway. This is her after-work spot. It's the hippest place in Rittenhouse. Since Violet, Colt, Rocco, and I—and now Nate, I guess—live within six blocks, it's where we meet. The Pearl has great food and a good drink menu. Lots of craft beers. I would prefer somewhere lower profile, but I'm outnumbered.

When Rocco suggested the Pearl for Nate's first night in Philly, I knew there was no way to avoid this. I just... I don't know. I wanted to prepare her or shield her. Something.

The crowd parts as if they're not stupid enough to get in her way. Violet Tannehill is a force of nature. Tonight, it's clear she's come straight from the office. In a black pencil skirt, white flowy blouse, and spiky black heels, she's a fucking wet dream. Her hair's partially up, but most of it is loose around her shoulders, a waterfall of blond waves. What remains of red lipstick is on her mouth, and it should look unkempt. It doesn't, though. She's the most beautiful girl I've ever seen. I think that every time I see her, whether it's been a day or a week since the last time.

Right now, though, she wears the fake smile I hate. "Hey, guys," she says, the epitome of breezy sophistication. She leans in to hug

Colt. "We're all sitting in the crow's nest." She points to the balcony that overlooks the main bar floor.

I brace myself, as I always do when she wraps her arms around my neck to hug me. Her scent, some perfume by Burberry, assails me, and I shift to hide my body's reaction. She doesn't notice. I've been doing the same shift since we met in our junior year in college.

She rises onto her tiptoes. When she speaks in my ear, the feel of her breath against my neck is a torturous ache. "What's he doing here?"

"Your phone's dead, isn't it?" I say back.

Her gaze meets mine briefly, and I know I'm right. As she pulls away, I adjust my enormous body so I'm between her and Nate. It's the slightest change. I doubt anyone else notices it.

Violet offers Nate her false smile. "Nate. What a surprise. I didn't know you were in town."

Next to me, it's clear Nate's shell-shocked. Is he star-struck by Violet too? I wouldn't blame him, but it pisses me off.

"Violet?" he asks, as if he isn't sure she's real.

I grit my teeth. Of course, it's Violet. She's pretty enough to be a fucking supermodel. It's hard to mistake her for anyone else.

"I didn't know... I mean, you're here. In Philly," he says.

Her smile is almost pitying. "Yes." She squeezes my hand, and then motions toward the stairs. I miss her fingers when she lets go. "Come on. We'll pull up some extra seats. The guys already ordered some apps."

She heads through the crowd again, and more than a few guys follow her with their gaze. When they catch me watching them, they look away. Good.

Nate catches my arm. "You didn't tell me Violet was in town."

"Violet's here. Does it matter?" I ask, lifting my brows. Because it shouldn't matter. He had his chance with her. Fucked it up royally.

"I mean, no. Well, maybe. I don't know." He stares after her.

"Right. Come on." Clenching my hands into fists, I follow her through the bar. It's satisfying that people move out of my way, too, and I get my fair share of appreciative glances—if I cared about random women's stares, which I don't.

It's hot in the crow's nest, and I press my glasses up on my nose. Violet's coworkers have the prime tables farthest from the stairs. Violet makes introductions and slides onto a stool with a red blazer and leather tote hanging on the back. I pull out a seat next to Violet, and Olivia arranges herself next to Nate. I'm not surprised to see her head straight for the fresh meat.

A server takes our drink orders. Next to me, Violet doesn't say much. She's all smiles, and she answers when asked direct questions, but she's usually the center of conversation. When it's clear she's not eating the nachos in front of her, I dig in.

I wait until the rest of the table is distracted, and then I lean in and whisper, "I texted you."

She nods. "My phone died at the office."

"I figured," I say. She casts me a droll glance, and it's the first time tonight she's like her usual self. I smile at her. "What? I'm just saying if your phone was a plant you needed to water, it would die."

"I could keep a plant alive." She swipes a nacho and crunches into it, glaring at me. "I have reminders on my phone for stuff like that."

"The phone that's always dead?" I lift my brows, teasing her.

Her laugh is like cool air on the hottest day, and it soothes the worry I've felt since I found out I would have to babysit Nate tonight. Across the table, I catch Nate watching her. I grit my teeth.

Pointing at her nachos, I ask, "This your dinner?"

She shrugs. "We had hoagies at the office earlier."

"Good, huh?"

She wrinkles her nose. Violet hates lunchmeat.

"Eat a little more." I push the plate toward her.

She scowls as she picks up a nacho coated in processed cheese. "Bossy," she says with a wink.

"Spacey," I fire back.

It's a running joke between us. When we met, she said I was antisocial because I don't say much. I thought she was an airhead sorority girl. I still don't say much, and when I do, I use as few words as possible. Admittedly, I can come off rough, so I own my bossiness. But Violet is no ditz. She flakes out because she's watching everything and everyone all the time. She's the most observant person I know. And when she's distracted by paying attention to everything else—like now—someone needs to take care of her. That's where I come in.

"What's he doing here?" she asks under her breath between bites, her face averted. "You guys aren't playing them, are you? I thought Denver was in a different conference."

"It is." We don't play a lot of the western teams. "He got traded."

She covers her mouth, sputtering. I hand her a glass of water. She shakes me off and reaches for her drink, downing the end—an old-fashioned. It must have been a rough workday.

"Traded?" she finally says.

I nod. "To take over for Huck."

"Right. For Huck." She inhales a deep breath and pushes her plate away before addressing the table. "You guys, it's been a long day. I think I'm going to head home." She spins her stool, sliding gracefully onto her spiky heels, her smile firmly in place. "I just need to visit the ladies' room. Excuse me."

She's gone before I can say anything. I watch her head toward the restrooms, her spine straight and her pace unhurried. It takes all my strength to stay seated and not follow her. But I know her—she needs a minute to pull it together.

At the other end of the table, Nate stands. "Are the restrooms in the back?" he asks, pointing in the direction Violet just went. He heads that way before anyone can confirm.

When I glance down, my knuckles are white where they grip the table. I force myself to loosen my hold.

Next to me, Lyle sips his beer before nudging his head after them. "What's up with the new guy?"

I cast a sideways look at him. He couldn't give two shits about Nate. He's had a thing for Violet since the summer.

I don't mince words. "They used to date. When we were in college." My drink arrives, and though I have a game tomorrow, I take a long pull. "He's the Tyrants' new goalie."

Lyle's eyebrows disappear under his expensive haircut. "As usual, Hunter, you're a fount of information."

I lift my shoulder in a half-shrug, smothering my humorless smile with another sip. From where I sit, I watch the hallway to the restrooms, debating my options.

Every muscle in my body wants to follow them. But Violet's not mine. We're only friends. She's also the most independent person I know. Macho manning in there, trying to save her, would only piss her off—she isn't a damsel in distress. So I sip my beer and do my best not to stare daggers after them.

Violet

After I wash my hands, I stare hard at my reflection. *Weak, Tannehill.* I square my shoulders and nod. Sure, I didn't expect to see Nate here. In fact, I planned to avoid him for the rest of my life. I figured it wouldn't be hard. We don't have a lot of chances to cross paths. I'm a junior financial analyst, and he's a professional hockey player living across the country. Or he used to live across the country, I guess.

Traded to Philadelphia. Just my luck. Well, avoiding him just got harder unless I want to cut ties with Hunter, and that's not an option. Nate might have had the power to break my heart a year ago, but I'm not that girl anymore. He has no influence over me, and he won't keep me away from my closest friend.

I snag a paper towel, dry my hands, and crumple it. After tossing it into the trash, I open the door... to find Nate waiting for me.

"Violet. Hey. Long time no talk," he says with a charming grin.

He pushes away from the wall, opening his arms wide. Does he think I'm going to hug him? If he does, he's lost IQ points since we dated.

Objectively, he's better looking than he was in college. He's still the same height and build and is in great shape, of course. But he's more polished. His hair isn't as unruly as it used to be, and his clothes... well, someone finally taught him how to dress. When we were together, he was athletic-wear chic all the way. Right now, he's in khakis and a button-up shirt, and I imagine lots of girls have checked him out since he got here. They're welcome to him.

"Yes. I still have the same number. Bet you do too." I want to roll my eyes, but I don't even know if it's worth it. I shift away from the entrance to the ladies' room to make room for two girls to get through. "Excuse me." I head back to the table, but he snags my hand, pulling me out of the flow of bar traffic. Stopping, I pull my fingers from his grip. "What do you want, Nate?"

"Violet, come on." He gives me the smile I remember from college, the one that used to melt me. Now it just seems calculated. "We used to be close. You're here, and I'm playing for the Tyrants."

"We're geographically adjacent. Yippee." I try to step around him again, but he shifts, cutting me off.

"I just mean..." His eyes scan the room as if searching for words in the crowd. This conversation isn't going how he expected, I assume. "We used to be friends."

"Used to be. Yes." I nod, folding my arms. "We used to date too. And sleep together. We don't do any of those things anymore, and I sure don't want to talk to you." I don't like overt hostility, but I'm not one to shy away from it either. In my defense, he wasn't getting the message any other way.

He reaches for me again, but my stance is a closed door. He drops his hand along with the smooth facade. What remains on his face is more like the eager-to-please, goofy guy I remember. I didn't feel much for the man who walked in the bar, but this guy... he sparks nostalgia like nothing else. Or rather, he brings back memories of the girl I used to be. Sometimes, I miss her.

"Violet, I'm sorry for how we left things. I really am." This almost sounds genuine. "The way I ended everything was stupid. I was just... scared about graduating and moving away. Starting with Denver. I could have handled things between us so much better."

The words are unexpected, and I don't think I realized I needed to hear them. "You could have," I agree. "Thank you for saying that."

"Great. I'm glad we got that out of the way." His grin is boyish, just like I remember. But when he cups my shoulders and pulls me into his arms, that's not what I expected.

I push against him, but it's like trying to disentangle myself from a boa constrictor. Hockey players are very strong, especially the dense ones. "Please let me go."

Suddenly, he does. Maybe it's the heels or because I chugged the rest of my old-fashioned, but I almost tip over. A hand presses into my lower back, holding me up as I recover my balance. That's when I find Hunter with a fist full of Nate's shirt next to me.

"What the hell, Nate?" he growls. "She almost fell over."

Nate lifts his hands. "Whoa, Hunt. Just hugging an old friend."

"She didn't want a hug." Hunter's mouth barely moves when he grits out the words.

He looks pissed, and that might have surprised me at any other time because Hunter rarely gets mad. But right now, I'm mostly preoccupied by the feel of his fingers splayed across my back. I can feel the warmth of them through my silky blouse, and it feels so... good. I mean, of course, it does. Because Hunter's my friend, and he's looking out for me, like always. That must be why I'm so aware of him touching me.

Nate's brows lower, and he shoves Hunter in the chest. It's not a hard push. Both of them are huge and strong enough to drop someone if they want to. This was only a warning. "What's your deal? This isn't your business, Mason."

Everything about Hunter tightens—his jaw, his shoulders, his entire stance—even though his hand stays firmly on the small of my back. This is a dangerous situation. Hunter and Nate used to be like brothers, and now Nate's on his team. Sure, I didn't want to hug Nate. I never want to touch him again. But right now, the two of them ooze testosterone. Whatever happens next could drive a wedge between them or cause problems at their job.

"Actually, it is his business," I say, stepping between them. Hunter increases the pressure on my back, trying to move me out of the way. I glare at him, standing my ground.

"It is?" Confusion colors Nate's features, like he's trying to figure out a puzzle. In college, I used to think his cluelessness was endearing. Now I wonder how I ever thought he was anything but dense.

"It is?" Hunter repeats beside me. I glance up at him, and he wears the closed look I hate, the one that makes it impossible to read him.

"Yes, of course." I smile at him with gritted teeth, and then I wind my arm around his waist. The move pulls me flush against his side. I can feel every ripped line of him. Has he always felt like that? "Because Hunter and I are dating."

Hunter

She's lost her fucking mind.

Dating, dating, dating... the word ricochets through my brain. It doesn't compute, especially with her body pressed against mine, so I repeat what she said. "We're dating."

She squeezes, and the pressure of her fingers at my hip is a jolt of electricity. "Yes." She slips out of my grasp, reaching for my hand. Her palm fits perfectly in mine. "I'm sure we'll run into each other, Nate, but I'm ready to go home." She looks up at me with a pleading expression. "Will you walk me, babe?"

"Absolutely." I always walk her home anyway, so it's not like she needs to ask. Next to us, Nate looks completely lost.

She tugs my hand, and together, we head back to the table. When we get there, she shrugs into her red blazer and slings her tote over her shoulder. No one else can probably see the tension in her when she smiles.

"See you guys tomorrow?" she asks her coworkers. A couple of them grumble but nod. She offers Colt a wave. "Good luck tomorrow." Then, without another word, she heads for the stairs.

I salute the table. Jonathan touches his eyebrow, and Lyle waves me off. I catch Nate watching us as I follow Violet downstairs.

We don't talk until we hit the pavement outside the Pearl. I need to jog to catch up with Violet. She's squeezing the halves of her blazer together against the November chill, but I bet the pace she's keeping on her heels is keeping her warm.

When I'm beside her and out of sight of the bar, I catch her sleeve. "Violet, what the hell?"

She stops and spins on me. "I know, I know," she wails, brushing her hair out of her face. "What was I thinking?" When she gets upset, the faintest hint of Texan comes out in her voice. I've always found it adorable, but now I also kind of want to shake her. "That was so stupid."

"Well, it wasn't as smart as you usually are—that's for sure," I concede.

"It's just, you were going to get firm with him, and I didn't want you to say something that would screw up your job. You guys need to work together. But I also didn't want him to think he could just..." She blows out an irritated breath. "Act like we were the same or even close to the same or even right at all."

Her rambles are picking up speed, and that's never a good sign, so I lift my hands. "All right, it's going to be fine."

"How's it fine?" She glares at me like I'm the one who got us into this.

I shrug helplessly. "I don't know."

She throws her arms up and paces away. As I watch her, I force myself to slow my racing thoughts and tackle this logically. I'm the oldest of six kids. In my experience, panic never helps.

"Okay, let's just look at this," I say. She stops again and props her hands on her hips, scowling at me. I can't help but grin. "There are worse things than someone thinking you're dating me." I mean it to sound joking and light, but the words make my heart clench. Because dating Violet is what I've wanted for months—more than a year, maybe.

"I know that." She waves me off.

"Half our friends think we're already dating. You know that, right?" It's impossible to miss the nudges and knowing looks.

She shrugs. "I know. And you're great. It's just that we would never date."

Something ugly twists in my stomach. I laugh, but it's self-deprecating. "That's right. Friends for us."

She nods and gives me a smile that dazzles me. "Exactly. Friends is better."

Usually, when we even get close to this topic, I leave it alone. But tonight feels different. Something about having her declare us together a few minutes earlier makes it feel more important to hear the truth.

"Why's that again?" I cross my arms in an attempt to brace myself. Whatever she says is going to dig like a knife inside me—I'm certain of it.

Her face becomes serious. "Because you're a forever kind of guy. And I'm a 'see you never' in the morning kind of girl."

We don't talk about who we date, and hearing her talk about one-night stands sends a possessiveness I don't deserve to feel streaking through me. I'm an idiot. Of course, she sees people. She's gorgeous and one of the most affectionate people I know. I guess I've always known she would have something going on, but she always kept it away from me.

I already hate the nameless guys she sees. But she's always been clear—we're friends. And as much as I want to deny what she says,

I can't. I'm not a forever guy with anyone else. But I could never be casual with Violet.

"Why did you jump in with him, anyway?" She props her hands on her waist. "I had it."

"What exactly in our acquaintance makes you think I'd let anyone disrespect you?" I fire back. "Especially Nate."

All the bluster leaves her, and she reaches forward to squeeze my arm. "I know." She sighs. "I'm so sorry if I dragged you into something awkward."

I shrug. Because I don't care if it's awkward. I've never cared much about what people think of me, and I don't plan to now. No, what's hard is that I want what she suggested. I want it so much it hurts.

"I'll fix it," she adds, swiping strands of flyaway blond hair out of her eyes as she squeezes her blazer closer around her. It's too cold to stand out here. I motion toward the sidewalk, and she nods, heading toward her apartment. As we set off, I match her shorter strides. Violet's a tall girl, but she's wearing heels, and I'm a giant.

"Yeah?" I grin. "You already planning to break up with me?"

She blinks up at me, almost tripping. I steady her without missing a step, and she continues. "You could break up with me if you want."

I laugh. "As if anyone would believe that." Only an idiot would break up with Violet Tannehill. That's probably why I've lost so much respect for Nate. She loved him, and he wasn't smart enough to see how precious that was.

"What's that supposed to mean?" She almost sounds offended. This whole situation is completely bonkers.

I shake my head. "Nothing. It's not hurting anything. You can just break up with me or decide we're just friends again whenever you want. Just let me know."

"We are friends, though."

"Exactly."

I can feel her gaze on me, but I don't make eye contact. I don't trust what she might see on my face. Finally, she sighs. "You're confusing, Hunt."

I tuck my hands in my pockets. "Feeling's completely mutual, Vi."

We walk the rest of the way to her apartment building in silence. She starts up the stairs and stops on the second one before turning back and throwing her arms around me in a hug. She pulls away quickly, though. A definite friend hug. "I really am sorry. We'll call it off soon. I swear it won't affect you at all."

Reaching forward, I button the two buttons on her blazer. My voice is gruff when I say, "No rush."

"You're not seeing anyone, are you?" Her eyes widen. "I didn't even think how this could affect your actual love life. If you are—"

"I'm not seeing anyone," I assure her.

She nods. "Okay. Good. I mean, not because you're not seeing anyone. I want you to be happy. But I wouldn't want to cause you any trouble—"

"Violet, I get it." I don't want to listen to her explain away how she wants me to be happy with someone else. That would just be the croutons on top of this shit salad. "Good night."

"Right. Good night." She pauses in front of the door the doorman still holds open. "Good luck tomorrow. I'll text you."

I wave, and she scurries inside. I wait until the door closes behind her before I walk away.

Violet

As soon as I'm locked in my apartment, I head straight for the shower. Bars smell weird, and I can't sleep with that in my hair. After I'm out, I want to go right to bed. I'm exhausted. It's been a long week, and I had a couple of drinks. I should be ready to pass out.

But I know myself. My brain spins, and I won't be able to sleep yet. Instead of climbing into bed, I head into my spare bedroom and sit down at my computer.

My friend June stayed with me for a bit recently, but besides that, I've never had a roommate. Not at college and not here. In college, I opted for a single all four years, despite the additional cost, because I suffered through periods of insomnia. Sometimes I sleep great. Other times, I'll only get a few hours here or there. I never wanted to bother someone else with my chaotic rest patterns.

Right now, I can tell I'm not ready to lie down. I boot up the program I'm working on. Coding makes me happy. It's just numbers and math, and I've always loved both.

Right now, I'm working on a dessert project. It was inspired by our current client. I keep feeling like their reporting platform is missing a few fundamental pieces in their portfolio setup. At night, when I can't sleep, I let my brain try to fix their problem.

But ten minutes later, my programming isn't doing what I need it to do. I need it to distract me from everything that happened at the bar and after with Nate and Hunter.

After five more pointless minutes, I shut the computer down. After turning off the light, I return to my bedroom and plop down on my bed, reaching for my headphones. When I've got soothing music going, I close my eyes and hope my brain calms.

It doesn't. What surprises me most is that I keep coming back to Hunter's face after I hugged him at my door. Usually, he's the picture of stoicism—reserved, steady all the time. But tonight, there was something in his expression that looked a little like longing and a lot like resignation. Whatever it was, I didn't like how it made me feel one bit.

I wonder what made me tell Nate that Hunter and I are together? More important, why am I lying on my bed, wondering what that would actually be like? Unable to lie still, I get off the bed and pace the length of my room.

Hunter is my best friend. I have a lot of acquaintances and some close friends, but none of them have ever been there for me the way he has. When I talk, I can tell that he's listening. And I talk a lot. Sometimes there's so much going on in my brain I feel like it'll explode if I don't just let it out.

It sounds so simple, but it's not. At least, I've never met another person who is quite that attentive to me. When we hang out, we talk. He might not say much, but when he talks, it's important and insightful.

He sees me. Not just the former pageant girl, the pretty face. He gets me. When Nate and I broke up, I wasn't even sure I got me.

Hunter was my anchor. Even if I wasn't sure who I was, he always seemed to know.

My mom had me on the pageant circuit when I was barely walking. I won a few, and people treated me like I was special. When I learned to sing, people noticed. The pastor's wife asked me to sing at church. Everyone said it was beautiful.

I was always a straight-A student, but that didn't turn people's heads like my looks or my voice did. It wasn't something I noticed until high school, and my mother became more obsessed with my debutante debut than my grades. The day she told me I should hide how smart I was because "men don't like brainy women" was the day I learned I needed to keep my curiosity hidden from her as well. Oh, she was fine if I was interested in society, in the happenings at my father's country club. She definitely wanted me to get good grades, too. I needed to be smart—just not too smart.

I figured out I could pursue my nerdy endeavors as long as I balanced them with her socially acceptable ones. To join the robotics team, I made the cheerleading squad first. I traded student council for the math club. After I made homecoming court, I applied to a coding intensive class at UT at Austin. It was exhausting.

When I applied to colleges, I chose Chesterboro University in eastern Pennsylvania. They offered an accelerated dual degree in conjunction with Penn. I walked away from four years there with a double major in finance and computer engineering. I also joined Delta Alpha, my grandmother's sorority, and became the vice president of finance. That pacified my mother. It surprised me how happy it made me too. If it hadn't been for Delta, I wouldn't have met Nate.

He was the exact guy my mother would have picked—so handsome, from a well-connected Boston family. Plus, the Chesterboro hockey team was one of the best in the country. When I dated him, I felt like I could have everything—not only a satisfying career, but a relationship my parents approved of. For the first time, something that made me happy could make my family happy, too.

Our breakup hit hard, a red mark on the possibility that I could have it all. I still haven't sorted the fallout from that failure. That was probably part of the reason I stumbled so badly this evening, telling Nate I was with Hunter.

Shaking my head, I flop back down, squeezing my eyes shut again. I'm a disaster. Even thinking about what it would be like to really date Hunter is irresponsible. I need to stay on course—focus on my job—and forget about dating anyone. My career is on track, and I plan to get promoted before my peers do. When I'm out of the newbie trenches, I'll learn everything I can about financial technology and move up the ladder at this company.

Maybe after I'm a super-successful businesswoman, I'll have the emotional capacity to date again. But right now, I need to come up with a way to call off this made-up relationship with as little fanfare as possible and get everything between us back to normal. The absolute last person I want to hurt is Hunter Mason.

Hunter

Before our game on Saturday night, Coach Hargreeves stops me. "Mason. Let's talk in my office."

"Sure, Coach." I do as he asks, but immediately, I'm on the alert. Most of the time, I stay under the radar. I work hard and do as I'm told. That decreases the chances that I spend one-on-one time with the head coach.

After I follow him to his office, he sinks into his chair behind the desk. "Why don't you pull the door closed and have a seat?"

I do, and as the door clicks shut, my mind races, wondering what I could have done wrong. A closed door? Definitely not good.

Not one to mince words, Coach dives right in. "The organization is considering trade options for a few of our hockey players. You're one of them."

My stomach drops. I'm not sure what I expected, but it wasn't this. I worked hard and was exceeding everyone's expectations. It's strange for them to target me.

I inhale a deep breath, reaching for calm. "Sir, can I ask why?"

Coach steeples his hands. "It's no secret we're in a rebuilding year, and Huck's injury has added new options to our board. Since you started, you've proved you can hack it at this level. You're a gritty player. You work hard. You're worth something on the market,

Mason. A lot more than you're getting paid now." He tilts his head. "Huck Sokolov is a legendary goalie, and he makes a legendary salary. If he can't play, it's time for us to move him to free up cap space. If we add your potential to the mix, we think we might piece together some interesting deals, deals that could be mutually beneficial to all involved."

I don't have a response to that. Apparently, Coach doesn't need one, because he continues. "I don't have control of all the details, but I called you in to find if there was anywhere you wanted to go?"

"Where?" I repeat.

"Yes. You're a young guy. Where would you be happy to be traded?" Coach lifts his hands. "There's no guarantee I'll be able to honor your request. But we try to take these things into account for our players, especially players who have been good to us."

I blink, my mind racing. I didn't expect this question in the first place, and I struggle to answer it. "If it's a possibility, I would prefer to be closer to my family."

Missouri is a long way from Philadelphia. I've been able to see my family twice since I moved here. I'm lucky. Lots of recent graduates far from home can't afford to get back to their families like I can. Even so, it would be nice to be within driving distance.

Coach Hargreeves nods as if he expected the answer. "That's a reasonable request. We'll see what we can do."

"Thank you."

"One other thing."

"Sir?"

Coach's expression gets apologetic.

Uh-oh...

"The organization sponsors the Sneaker Ball with the other major sports teams in town. We need players to attend, to draw attention to the charities it benefits." He shrugs. "You need to go. For the good publicity."

As soon as I heard the word ball, I started shaking my head. "Coach, please reconsider." I don't dance, and I hate huge gatherings. "Respectfully, this isn't my scene."

"It is if I'm trying to talk you up to other organizations. 'Team player,' I'll say. 'Involved in the local community.'" He lifts his hands. "Executives eat that shit up."

I want to roll my eyes, but I don't. Nothing about my upbringing would allow overt disrespect of authority. "Yes, sir."

"Buck up, Mason. Nate, Duke, and Colt all need to go as well."

I barely stifle my groan. If going to what is essentially a huge dance wasn't bad enough, spending extra time with Nate right now sends the situation into hellish territory. "Can I bring a guest?"

He nods. "You get a plus-one."

"Great." I'll get Violet to come. She was quick to insist we were dating last night, just in time for this. A grin tugs at my lips, and I suddenly feel lighter. "Thank you, Coach." I stand, preparing to leave.

"Mason?" Coach calls, stopping me at the door. When I glance back, he raps his knuckles on the desk. "This is a compliment, son. Take it as such."

I nod.

"Oh, and any trade talk in the organization is confidential until the publicity department releases it. So don't tell anyone."

"No problem, Coach."

"Now, get out there and win this game."

"Yes, sir," I say.

Leaving the door open because it's weird to see it closed, I head back toward the locker room, my head still spinning. I've only been part of the Philadelphia Tyrants organization for a few months, but I didn't plan to leave. As far as professional hockey players go, I don't make that much. It hasn't bothered me, though. I like my colleagues, get to play hockey for a living, and, well, I've been able to be with Violet. It's enough for me.

My thoughts race, but in the end, all I can focus on is Violet. If I get traded, I'll be far away from her. I've never pushed her for more. At first, after she broke up with Nate, I wanted to be there for her. Even though I wanted her, I didn't approach her because I didn't want to be a rebound. It was awkward because Nate was my friend. By the time the weirdness faded, I kept waiting for her to be ready. But Violet has shown no signs of being interested in a relationship. In fact, she's actively avoiding them. In college, she said she wanted to focus on her senior classes. That sounded legit. She was a double major and needed to take some classes at Penn. Since graduation, she's been busy with work and establishing her career. She might be busier than I am, and I'm a professional hockey player who travels and trains constantly.

If I get traded, I know in my gut that my chances of starting something with her will deteriorate. We both travel so much and are so busy with work. Add her gun-shy feelings about dating, and it'll be practically impossible to get out of the friend zone. I'm not sure I even have a shot now, but if I leave, I'll never know.

I can't think about this here, though. I have to be on the ice in half an hour, and I have a game to concentrate on. Worrying about how my time in Philadelphia with Violet might be limited will need to wait until later.

Violet

On Saturday, I stay late at the office. I check in on Hunter's game a few times. Though the score stays tied until the third period, Colt buries one with a few minutes left on the clock, and they hold on for the win. When I get home, I fall right into bed, exhausted, and manage six full hours of sleep.

I'm up early on Sunday, planning to do some more work at home. My mom calls before I have my coffee. I try not to groan as I answer, pouring my first cup. "Good morning, Mama."

"Violet, my darling. It's lovely to hear your voice." As always, my mother is perfectly upbeat. I'm probably the only one who hears the censure in her words.

Pouring some creamer into my mug, I take a seat at the island. "I've been working really long hours this week. I apologize for not calling you back."

"Of course. And I wouldn't dare keep you long, because I suspect you're very busy."

I want to point out that her calls are frequently long. But I don't think that'll help my cause. So I bite my tongue.

She continues. "I wanted to catch you before I leave for service, so we can finalize plans for the holidays."

That's right. Christmas is only a few weeks away. "I haven't had much time to think about it yet."

"Well, of course you'll be home." Her tone says it's outrageous to suggest otherwise.

"I suppose." I take a long sip from my mug. This conversation needs more caffeine. "It's just that Hannah and Cord are getting married on Christmas Eve, so I'll be in Chesterboro for that."

Both are good friends from college. Hannah Marshall is an up-and-coming musician, and her fiancé, Cord Spellman, plays for the New Jersey Jaguars. Their schedules have little overlapping time for special occasions like weddings. Hence, the holiday ceremony.

"After that, I'll need to figure out when I can fly to Austin," I say.

I know immediately the explanation won't be good enough for my mother, and her gasp validates me. "Violet Jean. You're our only daughter. Of course, you'll be home during the holidays."

I press my palm against my forehead and tuck the phone between my shoulder and my ear. "Mom, I need to clear the time off with my boss."

"Any respectable company would allow their employees to visit their families with enough notice."

I stop myself from pointing out that Dad's hedge fund also doesn't provide unrestricted vacation time. "I'll get as much time as I can. I'll definitely be there for New Year's Eve, Mom." I reach for a napkin and jot down a quick note to request the time when I log on.

"Oh, that would be wonderful," she exclaims, clearly pleased that she got her way. "I'm so glad. I miss you so much. We'll be having our annual New Year's party, of course."

Shaking my head and rolling my eyes, I can't help my grin. Because though my mother is forceful, she loves me. I don't doubt that she misses me, too, even though I've spent most of my life feeling like I haven't been able to live up to her expectations. "I'll definitely plan to attend the party, Mama. Would hate to miss it." When I say the words, I realize they're not a lie. It'll be nice to see familiar faces.

"Did I see Nate is in Philadelphia?"

My smile drains away. "How did you hear that?"

"Oh, you know. It was on the news or something."

Even though I'm thousands of miles away, I'm not surprised that my mother knows so many intimate details in my life. Still, it's alarming. "Right."

She doesn't seem to hear the distaste in my tone, or she purposely ignores it. "Have you seen him?"

"Mother..."

"You have, haven't you?" She practically squeals. "Now that you two are in the same town, the stars will align for you. You'll be back together before you know it. That's what I told Stephanie when I talked to her yesterday."

I should have known. Stephanie is Nate's mother. She and my mom became fast friends when they met during homecoming the year Nate and I were dating. "I'm sorry, Mom, but that won't happen."

"He made a mistake, darling. Some men just take longer to grow up, that's all."

"I'm not getting back together with Nate, Mom." I insert as much force into my voice as I can without sounding harsh. But I can't have her thinking there is even a possibility. When she gets something into her head, she is tenacious. I settle on the first thing I can think of. "I'm dating someone else."

As soon as the words are out, I close my eyes and pray for deliverance. It's the perfect thing to say if I want her to leave me alone about Nate. But it opens up a larger can of worms.

The pause on the line is heavy, especially because my mother is never without something to say. "You are?"

I've come too far now. "Yes. I am."

"Why haven't you said anything?" She almost sounds hurt.

"It's very new," I assure her. Yeah, like last-night-and-fake kind of new. "And I told you, it's been a very busy week." None of this is technically a lie. After all, Hunter and I did agree to fake date last night. And I did have a very busy week.

"Well, yes, but not even a text..." Her voice trails off. "Who is this new man?"

I brace myself. "It's Hunter."

"Hunter Mason? But, well, you two are only friends. Isn't that what you've said?"

"It is. I guess now we're more than friends."

I can practically hear the wheels turning in her mind as she pieces together everything she knows about him. There's probably a lot. Hunter and I have been friends for a while, and I talk about him all the time. I can hear the tally in her head, too. I wait for it.

"He's from Missouri, isn't he? His family is in agriculture." The way she phrases it makes them sound like they're white-collar, and they aren't.

I sigh. "Yes. His family farms." I say the words she won't.

Even though my mother's snobbery is predictable, it still bothers me. Hunter is one of the best people I've met, and his family is affectionate, supportive, and down-to-earth. I hate that my mother would judge them, knowing nothing about them.

I'm exhausted by this conversation. "Mom, I really need to get some more work done today."

"Bring him with you."

"What?"

"I said that you should bring Hunter home with you. For the holidays. So we can meet him."

"Mom, you've already met him." I scramble for more excuses. "It's still really new. I don't know if he can. He's on the Tyrants, remember? He might have a game—"

"For as little or as much as you can," she says, cutting me off. "Your father and I want to see you, and I want to meet him. To know what's going on with you."

I swallow and allow the guilt to wash over me. For my sake, I moved away from my parents. As I neared college graduation, I tried to imagine pursuing my dreams under their watchful eye. It seemed easier to stay in Pennsylvania than to return to Texas. But I know they miss me, and even though things are complex, I miss them too.

"I'll see what I can do."

"Wonderful. I'll be in touch over the next week."

"Sounds good. I love you, Mom."

"I love you more, Violet Jean."

We hang up, and I drop my head into my hand. I like to think I'm a smart girl. My grades and success at work and school would back me up. But when I get myself into these kinds of personal situations, I have to wonder. It was bad enough that I dragged Hunter into a fake relationship on Friday night. Now I've brought my mother into the debacle.

I would love to spend time with Hunter over the holidays. I assume he plans to go home to see his family if he can. They're very close, and I know he misses them. It means stretching our fake-dating arrangement until the new year. It's only a month, and Hunter said he didn't mind. But I've stayed up too late the last two nights, thinking about our arrangement. I've definitely spent way too much time remembering the feel of his fingers on my back.

I'll talk to him. Hunter always sees the heart of any matter. I'm sure together, we'll be able to smooth all of this over.

Determined, I pick up my phone and drop Hunter a text: *I'm going to order food tonight. Come over and eat it with me?*

His typing dots appear: *Be there at six.*

I smile, feeling lighter.

Hunter arrives five minutes early, and he brings red wine.

"You're a prince." I take the bottle and close the door behind him.

"That's what I keep telling you," he shoots back, kicking off his sneakers by the door before following me to the kitchen. He's in sweats and a thermal shirt. The baggy clothes do nothing to hide the mountain of muscle he is. He pushes his glasses up on his nose. "It smells delicious in here."

I point toward the stove, where I left the takeout containers of Chinese food. "Help yourself."

He knows where the plates and silverware are because he's here so often, so I don't help him. That's one of the nice things with Hunter—everything is so comfortable. I never have to pretend with him.

He fills up his plate, and I open the wine. "Do you want some?" I ask.

He shakes his head. “Nah. Early flight to Vancouver.”

Nodding, I put the cork back on the top as he sits on his usual island stool. I have a table for eating, but most of the time, it feels too formal to sit there with him, so we usually hang here. Snagging my full wine glass, I sit across the counter from him, like always.

He pauses as he shovels food into his face, his fork halfway to his mouth. “You not eating?”

“I actually ate a bunch of popcorn and crackers an hour or so ago during a work break.” I lift my wine glass. “This is all I need right now.”

He points his fork at me. “Popcorn and crackers aren’t a real dinner. And neither is wine,” he adds when I take a sip. “Make sure you eat food.”

“Bossy,” I say even as I grin. Because it wouldn’t be the first time I forgot to eat. I take another sip. “Thanks for the wine. I needed a glass.”

“PLG?” he asks, lifting his eyebrows. I’ve filled him in on what a nightmare this client is.

I shake my head. “My mother.” He laughs because he also knows how different my mother and I are. “She wants me to come home over the holidays,” I say.

“That sounds nice. You’re going to Cord and Hannah’s wedding, though, aren’t you?” Hunter played hockey with Cord and has an invitation to the wedding as well. We planned to drive out together.

“Of course. She wants me to be there for New Year’s Eve. My family has an annual party, and I told her I’d be there for it.”

“Is it fun?”

“It is,” I admit. “My mother knows how to throw a party. But she also found out about Nate being in town.” His eyes meet mine, and he hums as he chews to acknowledge he heard me. I take a deep breath. "She thinks we should get back together."

It's only because I know him so well that I notice he stills, even stops chewing. After a moment, he swallows, putting his fork down. I watch him try to find something to say. Finally, he says, "Your parents really liked Nate, didn't they?"

We've never really talked about this. I nod. "His parents are Boston attorneys. Very involved."

"Right." He glances away. "Society types. That sounds like something your mother would like." It's a valid assessment, but it still makes me cringe.

"Yeah." I hate talking about stuff like this with him. Chesterboro is an expensive private school. There were lots of rich kids there, but Hunter attended on a sports scholarship, helped along by excellent grades. It always feels weird when our different backgrounds come up.

He appears to choose his words carefully again. "She has always wanted you to end up with someone wealthy and important."

I wince. It's a fact, and he could have definitely said it in a meaner way. But it still sours my stomach. "Yeah." I don't want to dwell on how perfect she thinks Nate was for me, so I wave that off. "It doesn't matter, though. Because I told her you and I are dating."

He sits up straighter, his eyebrows disappearing under his shaggy hair. "You did?"

"Yeah." I can't read his reaction, and that unsettles me, so I hurry on. "I don't know why. I guess... after I told Nate we were dating, and then she brought him up, well, it just slipped out again, I suppose. So then she invited you to come to New Year's Eve, to stay with my family. And I would love to see you and hang out with you. The party is a lot of fun. But I know you probably want to spend time with your own family since you don't see them much. And that is completely fair—"

He lifts his hand, and I'm grateful because I was just winding myself up and I don't know what else I would have said. He offers me a smile. "Violet. I'll check with my family, but I don't see any reason I can't come for New Year's Eve if you need me."

I exhale slowly and take another bracing gulp of my wine. "I shouldn't have lied to her. But she sounded so excited Nate was here... I didn't want to hear that." I reach across the counter for the open bottle and pour myself another glass. "And I definitely don't want to hear about it when I get home."

Hunter clears his throat. "Well, I actually was going to ask you for a favor, too. As part of your fake-girlfriend duties. The Tyrants are a sponsor for the Sneaker Ball this weekend. Coach says I need to go."

My heart skips a beat. "A ball?" That sounds like something out of a fairy tale. Unlike Hunter, I love getting dressed up.

Hunter nods, running his hand over his hair. "Yeah, it's for charity. I have to be there for work, and he said I could bring a date." He holds his hands up. "Before you agree, you should know that Nate's going as well."

Some of the excitement of getting all cuted up dulls. *Stupid ex-boyfriend*. "Ugh."

"Yeah. Apparently, the organization wants him to get his face out there. It sounds like they expect him to be a fixture on the team long-term, not just while Huck recovers." He shrugs. "I would appreciate it if you came with me. You know I suck at this stuff."

"Of course, I'll go with you." I wave my hand. "And anyway, it's not that I care about being around Nate. I don't. I don't have feelings for him anymore. But seeing him the other night…" I struggle to find the right words. "It reminded me how stupid I was."

Hunter's face storms over. "You weren't stupid."

"Stop." I laugh. The last thing I want to do right now is rehash my relationship with Hunter. I know he'll stick up for me, but I also know what really happened. Nate told me he loved me, but he never made me any promises. It was all me assuming we were a forever thing when we weren't.

He continues to scowl at me. "Nate Graham was a fucking moron."

My heart swells. It's probably not nice that he's talking about his former friend and current teammate like that, but I appreciate his support.

"Maybe," I allow. "Anyway, it sounds great. I'd love to go."

"Good. Because I already told them you were coming with me," he says, grinning.

I roll my eyes at his presumptuousness, but the wine's making me feel warm and content. "Because I'm your fake girlfriend?" I tease.

"No, because you're Violet." His face is sober, and any attempt to joke dies on my lips.

Hunter doesn't get like this—all serious—often. Usually, I feel like I amuse him. Or make him happy. Something. But when he gets like this, it makes my stomach flip. Almost like I'm falling, the same scary and exhilarating mix of emotions. And I never know exactly how to respond.

I divert my gaze and down the last of my wine. "Well, if we drag this out until Hannah and Cord's wedding on Christmas, we've got built-in dates for everything. Not really fake dating, I guess. More like plus-one with an asterisk." Still not meeting his eyes, I stand.

"But if you're going to be my boyfriend with an asterisk, Hunter Mason, we need to look convincing in public."

I hazard a glance at him, and the seriousness is gone. Instead, his face is a mask of alarm. His hands are in front of him like he plans to ward me off. "Wait. I know that look, Vi. I don't know what you're planning—"

"We need to learn how to dance." I move away from the island, opening my arms wide in the center of the living room, where there is enough space to move.

He scowls at me from his seat. "I can dance."

I cast him an incredulous look. "Hunt, I've danced with you before. I know the truth." Every time we've tried to dance, he's so stiff—it's like he's waiting for me to attack him. "We won't convince anyone we're together if we can't put on a better show than that. Definitely not my mom." I wrinkle my nose. When he still hesitates, I drop my hands to my hips. "Come on. I promise I won't jump you."

I head to the television stand, plug my phone into my speaker system, and search for the right song. Something to dance to. When I rejoin him in the middle of the room, some war is taking place on his features. Finally, he nods and steps in front of me.

Something about the way he looks at me is different, but I can't put my finger on it. As soon as he closes the distance between us, I wonder if I made a terrible mistake. Hunter uses one hand on my waist to pull me close and the other to cocoon my fingers. My heart picks up as I drop my hand to grip his shoulder, and our eyes meet. Heat streaks through me, settling in my stomach. *What the hell?*

He leans forward, lowering his face next to my ear. I breathe in the smell of him. His voice is rough and low.

"Let's make it convincing, then." He presses more firmly against me, and we move.

Hunter

As I take Violet in my arms, warning alarms go off in my head.

She wasn't lying. We've danced lots of times, usually when she's goofing around or we're drinking. But this time is different. Usually, when we're close, I worry I'll give myself away, so I brace myself. I try not to look at her, try not to even breathe. But yesterday's conversation with Coach and the looming possibility of a trade weigh on me.

I've always assumed my feelings were one-sided and that while I was always intensely aware of every touch, she felt nothing. She has always said we're only friends and we could never date, and I respected that. I've never let myself find out anything different. But tonight, I need to know.

Maybe I should be content with the status quo like she is. She's my best friend, and I don't want to screw that up. But I can feel my time with her running out, like sand in an hourglass. If there's a chance, if there could be anything between us, I want to know—one way or the other.

So tonight, with my heart pounding in my ears, I take her in my arms, and I let myself feel. She probably doesn't realize she gasps when our bodies come together. I can feel her pulse racing where my thumb presses against her slender wrist, and I can hear it echoing in the shallow breaths she takes. She picked something slow, and I guide us into a basic box step. God, she feels amazing in my arms and her fucking perfume… it's a heady buzz.

I move us around the room, and I can't look away from her face. My body cradles hers, and I continue to hold her even when the music stops. When our eyes meet, hers are dilated. She licks her lips, and at the sight of her tongue… fuck, I stifle a groan. That's the stuff of my wildest dreams. My body is immediately hard, and it takes everything in me to keep from pulling her closer, holding her tighter… dropping my mouth to cover her damp lips.

But while all signs point to desire, I know Violet, and I see the confusion and wariness in her expression. Worse, there's something else there… something that almost looks like fear. So even while my body screams for her, her fear hits me in the center of the chest. I can't stand it.

I step back but continue to hold her hand, not wanting to give up that last touch. Rubbing my thumb against the back of it, I try for an easy smile. My gruff voice probably gives me away, though. "I think we're going to be okay, don't you?"

Her eyes are wide, Violet clears her throat. "Dancing?"

A strand of hair came out of the bun on the top of her head. I push it behind her ear. "Pretending to be into each other."

"Oh." She nods too fast. "Yeah."

She looks so deliciously flustered that I need to retreat. I've definitely pushed this as far as I want to tonight. Dropping her hand, I jut my thumb toward the door. "I should go. Early flight."

"Right. Of course." She wraps her arms around herself and glances around, looking lost. Finally, she says, "Do you want any more of this food? There's so much."

Every instinct in me wants to stay, to soothe her—to help her figure out what's confusing her. But this won't be something I can do for her. I shake my head, slipping into my sneakers. "No, I'm good." After shrugging into my jacket, I reach for the door. "I'll talk to you tomorrow, Vi."

I practically run down the stairs from Violet's apartment. When I hit the street, the cool air helps. But I still need to bury my hands in my pockets to keep from clenching and unclenching my fists. I hurry the last blocks and bound up the stairs to the front door of my apartment building. After I key in the code, I stride down the hall to my door and let myself into my place.

A lot of the guys sublet rooms with other players. I did that initially, but when I signed on during training camp, my first order of business was finding my own space. I need my privacy. The studio I found is small, but it has everything I need. I don't like a lot of clutter, and my wardrobe is minimal. It works for me.

My body buzzes, the heat from that dance still racing through me, so I take a cold shower. It helps to calm my raging lust, but my brain still spins. So I pack for tomorrow's flight to Vancouver. When that's done, I sit on my bed. Staring at my luggage, I force myself to revisit my evening rationally.

Every sign from our dance screams that Violet feels something between us, too. Her softened body, her breathing, and her mouth... I'm no monk. I've read desire on women's faces before. But it's never hit me as hard as when I saw it develop on Violet's. Watching her get turned on fired me up.

I shake my head, dropping my face in my hands and pressing the heels of my palms into my eye sockets. In the past, I wondered if I glimpsed signs that Violet hadn't friend-zoned me as hard as she thought she had. Sometimes, I would catch her watching me, or her eyes would linger on my body for a little too long. I never let myself get my hopes up, though.

Because attraction isn't enough. I knew that before tonight, and nothing has changed.

I sigh and push to stand, needing to move. My place is small, so I end up pacing the length of it. She cares about me. She trusts me, too. Why else would she know I would go along with her declaring we were dating? She knows I've got her back, and realizing she depends on that has always made me feel like a superhero. Violet Tannehill doesn't lean on anyone else, but she will let me take care of her and watch out for her. I know that's a gift. And it has to mean something, right?

I just need to take it slow and give her time to figure it out. But not too slow, because I'm running out of time. A trade could come through any day. Slow but fast, I guess. That makes perfect sense. I roll my eyes at myself.

I have the Sneaker Ball next weekend. She'll think it's fun. She loves dressing up, and that's the perfect opportunity to act like we're together. Maybe it'll show her how good we would be as a real couple. Then, on Christmas Eve, we'll be in Chesterboro for Hannah and Cord's wedding, and then I'll go to Austin to be with her on New Year's Eve. Bonus: we'll be pretending to be a pair the entire time.

Those are lots of opportunities to win her over. So from here on out, it's time I make my move. With any luck, Violet's going to see how good we are together by the time the ball drops at the New Year's Eve party.

Violet

By Wednesday morning, it's apparent I won't be able to get a new dress for the Sneaker Ball, not because I don't want to but because I don't have any time. I worked fourteen-hour days Monday and Tuesday, and it looks like I'll be doing the same until the weekend, thanks to PLG. If we thought the project was a nightmare last week, it completely explodes this week.

I own lots of formal and cocktail dresses, but they're all in Austin at my parents' house. When I graduated, I didn't think I would have any need of them here in Philadelphia. I brought a few little black dresses with me, but they won't cut it for something like this ball. So I reach out for reinforcements and text my friend Penny Hampshire.

Penny and I were in the same sorority at Chesterboro University, and I hope she's got something that will work for me. We used to be the same size, though she's a little shorter. She's here in Philadelphia, too, at Temple Law.

She calls me a few hours later, but I can't answer because I'm putting out a work fire. When I call her back, she doesn't bother with small talk. "The Sneaker Ball, huh?" She whistles softly. "That's pretty fancy. How did you get invited to that?"

I hoped to avoid this part of the conversation. "Hunter. I'm his plus-one."

Penny squeals, and her tone turns teasing. "So, things are finally progressing with him?"

I pause as I type out an email. "What do you mean?"

"He invited you to one of the fanciest galas in Philadelphia. Doesn't that mean you're dating?"

Do I tell her the truth? It negates the point of fake dating if everyone knows it's fake. But this is Penny. She isn't going to tell anyone. "Well..." I say, buying time.

"You are!" She squeals. "I knew it."

I roll my eyes at her enthusiasm. "Penny, it's still very new."

"How can it be new if you guys have known each other forever?" She laughs. "I just knew it. You don't know how long all of us have been waiting for this."

My stomach drops. "What are you talking about?"

"Me, Shea, Cami. Ivy. Even Hannah," she says, rambling off the names of most of our closest friends from college. "And Hannah wasn't even on campus last year to watch you two together."

"Come on." I roll my eyes. "You can't be serious."

"Dead serious. We even had a poll." She seems to consider. "I lost last year, though."

"You thought we would get together last year?" I wrack my brain for anything about me last year that would indicate I was ready for a relationship. There's nothing.

"I hoped."

I can't think of anything to say. Hunter said our friends probably think we're together. Some part of me assumed they might consider it, but a whole poll devoted to it? That seems excessive.

"Anyway," she says, "I'm sure I have a few dress options for you. Short or long?"

"Short or cocktail, I guess?" I hadn't really thought about this yet. "The theme is sneakers, so if it's about the sneakers, I feel like people should see them."

I don't have any nice sneakers. I might need to order those. Penny and I might be the same size, but I'm taller, and my feet are bigger.

"Got it. Let me look, and I'll text you some pictures." She pauses. "Or we can get together for drinks over the next couple of days. I'd love to catch up."

"I would love to, but I'm swamped at work until our deadline on Friday." I tuck the phone between my ear and shoulder. "But maybe you can come over and help me get ready on Saturday. It'll be like old times." I smile, remembering doing each other's hair and makeup before formals in college.

"I'll bring snacks," she says, and relief floods through me.

"Thank you, Penny. You're a lifesaver."

As I hang up, I let out a deep sigh. I'm more nervous about this ball than I'd like to admit. Not because of the actual event—I've been to a lot of balls, even one with the governor of Texas. No, my anxiety is strictly Hunter-induced.

I keep revisiting the dance we had the other night. When I suggested it, I figured it would be fun, a way to defuse the tension between us. But the second he took me in his arms, I wondered if I made a terrible mistake.

He held my gaze, and no one has ever looked at me like that. Even days later, I can't figure out what it was about that look, but it made my heart pick up. It might have been the wine, but I keep remembering that his body felt perfect against mine where we touched. And the way he smelled... it should be illegal to smell like that. More importantly, why didn't I ever notice it before?

When we stopped, I had the strangest feeling. He stared at my mouth and his face... I could have sworn he wanted to kiss me. The craziest thing was... I think I might have wanted him to kiss me too. Which is a complete no-no. Hunter is out of bounds and always has been. It's too risky.

All those thoughts scrambled in my brain, and I couldn't think of anything to say. But then he was gone, leaving me standing in the middle of my living room, staring at the closed door, with the silence swallowing me.

What happened? I sit up straighter at my desk and press a hand to my forehead. Wine. That's what happened. Objectively, Hunter is ridiculously hot. And kind. It's a heady mixture, I'll admit. But if I hadn't been drinking, I'm sure the full force of it wouldn't have hit me in the belly the way it did.

Plus, I'm in the middle of a significant sex drought. The combination of booze and not getting laid must have had something to do with my body's reactions. That had to explain it.

I just won't drink at the ball. Sober as a nun. I'll be more capable of resisting unexpected hotness. That's the solution. Otherwise, I'll end up screwing up the best thing in my life right now, and that's not a risk I plan to take.

Hunter

THE TEAM FLIES HOME on Friday morning after away games on Tuesday and Thursday. Our Saturday game is at one o'clock, so it won't interfere with the Sneaker Ball that night. The flight leaves at dawn, so it's quiet, with most of us listening to music or sleeping.

Yesterday, Coach Hargreeves pulled me aside and said there's nothing concrete yet in any trade talks. I understand that these types of transactions can take time. I'm not an impatient guy. If it wasn't for Violet, I don't think I'd care how long things took or what happened at all.

I stare out the plane window and watch the sun rise. Except for a few texts, I haven't talked to Violet all week. Her project with PLG is ending today, so she's probably buried in work, but I miss her.

More, though, I'm worried our dance freaked her out. She doesn't seem freaked out in her texts—only busy. But Violet sometimes deflects when she's uncomfortable.

When we land, I snag my bag out of the overhead and make my way to the exit. Maybe I'll be able to see Violet for dinner. We have a meeting at the training center this afternoon, but I can probably get back to the city before too late. I pick up my pace.

I've got my AirPods in, so it isn't until I'm on the runway, walking toward the gate, that I notice Nate keeping pace beside me. He nods at me, and I pull one of my headphones out.

"Hey. I hear you're going to this party tomorrow night too," he says.

"Yeah. Sneaker Ball."

"Yeah." We match strides through the door and head down the corridor together. "I assume you're taking Violet with you."

It's not a question, but he waits for a response. I nod. "I am."

He chuckles, shaking his head. "I still can't believe you two are a thing."

My mouth thins. "Well, believe it or not, it's happening."

"Oh, don't get me wrong." He lifts his hands, all innocence. "She's great. A catch. But you two... you're so different. Just unexpected."

I'm going to regret this, but I ask anyway. "Why unexpected, Nate?"

Nate shrugs, burying his hands in his pockets. "I don't know, man. You've just always been the serious type, and she's... well, she's Violet. The party girl. Not serious at all. She's always the center of attention, outgoing. And you avoid the spotlight at all costs."

I try to mesh what I know about Violet with his description of her. He's not wrong, but he isn't right either. I force my face to stay impassive. "Just because we're different doesn't mean we can't be together. In fact, I think we balance each other out." I cast a glance at him. "Besides, Violet isn't the same person you dated. She's grown up. So have I." I want to mention that he should try it, but I'm not interested in being overtly hostile.

"No doubt, man. No doubt." He pauses, and I hope he's done. But then he says, "So, have you hit that yet?"

I stop walking and face him. "Excuse me?"

He shoves me on the shoulder, his face full of frat-boy stupid. "I mean, you guys have been together for a while now, right?"

My body flashes hot, and it takes everything in me to keep my cool. "This is none of your business, Nate. And if you like your face, never talk about Violet like that to me again."

"My bad." Nate holds up his hands. "I mean, she's hot. I know that better than anyone. But I get it. She belongs to you."

"She's not a possession, you dickhead. She's Violet." Was I ever friends with this guy? I can't believe it sometimes.

"Possession? Like in The Exorcist?" He looks around, clearly confused, and my anger seeps away, replaced by exasperation.

He's so simple. Like, four cents short of a nickel. I roll my eyes and head toward the exit.

The guy isn't getting the point, though, because he jogs to catch up with me. "You're right. That was out of line. It's none of my business," he says, and I give him a quick jerk of my head. "It's just so strange to see you two together. You... with Violet." He shakes his head. "Crazy."

"Well, maybe you just don't know her that well. If you did, maybe it would make more sense," I grit out. What does a guy need to do to be delivered from an awful conversation?

"Maybe you're right. Maybe she's different. But I don't know if people can change that much."

"And maybe you didn't know her that well in the first place," I shoot back.

"Maybe. I just don't want you to get hurt. A girl like her could chew you up and spit you out." He shrugs, and his smug-ass face makes me want to hit him. He lifts his hands in surrender. "You know what? I'll keep my thoughts to myself. This is done. I won't bring it up again."

"Good." I leave him there, keeping my eyes straight ahead. I head for the parking garage and my car.

When I click my key fob, the lights flash on my Tahoe, and it starts up. I slide into the front seat, tossing my bag onto the passenger side. While the engine warms, I grip the steering wheel, staring out into the early-morning light. Fucking Nate. I'm sure he got to me worse because I was already stressing about our dance and whether I overstepped boundaries or made her uncomfortable.

You two are so different. Just unexpected... He isn't wrong. At least, not completely. I have to admit that I'm so far gone for her that losing her could wreck me. And Violet and I are different. I'm no stranger to the idea that opposites attract, but I'm not sure they really stay together.

I scan the parking spaces, searching for some kind of answer. Nothing comes to me.

I shake my head. Violet and I might be different, but not in the ways it matters. I get how he sees her. When he and Violet got together, it wasn't serious at first. Violet was a party girl—no doubt about it. She was in a sorority, and she liked to have fun. We all did, though. We were in college. There was nothing wrong with that.

But the longer they stayed together, the clearer it was that she thought what was between her and Nate was more than just fun. She would talk about the future, about where they would be in years to come. I remember because it made me irrationally jealous. While he would agree with her, he rarely brought it up himself. I thought it was because graduation was creeping up and he didn't know where he would be playing. I assumed that when things solidified in his career, he would be fine. Everyone thought that, including Violet.

Because the more time I spent with Violet, the more I couldn't fathom that anyone in their right mind would willingly let her go. But although he signed a hockey contract and got a "real job," Nate didn't mature at all.

Violet did. She still likes to have fun and party, but she's invested in her career. I don't know anyone who works harder than she does. And she loves to be around people, but I would catch the way she would look at June when she was with Duke and his daughter, Tabby. Violet wants that too. Eventually. At least, that's what I've always assumed.

Am I right, though? She says she's not interested in relationships. That she wants to just focus on her career right now. Maybe I should take her at face value. Then again, she might not be interested if she knew how I felt. I don't know.

Should I tell her? Will I ever know anything if I don't?

Shaking my head, I shift into gear and navigate out of the parking garage. Tomorrow, when we're at the ball, I'll figure out a way to tell her. I don't know what's going to happen, but it's time to lay our cards on the table.

Violet

THANKS TO THE PLG account, I fell into bed early on Friday night. That didn't keep me from sleeping until after ten o'clock, though. Penny shows up at my place around noon on Saturday, and she brings me a bagel and my coffee—a latte with skim milk. I put Hunter's game on while we have brunch and catch up.

When Hunter scores, I cheer. Penny smiles at me, sipping from her to-go cup. "I'm still so excited to see you guys together."

Her genuine happiness on my behalf makes me uncomfortable, so I shake my head and wave her off. "I still think it's funny you guys were all betting on us."

She shrugs. "Then you two shouldn't be so cute together."

I think about that as I shower during intermission. Are we cute together? Probably. If I'm honest, we make a good team. Most good friends do.

Penny brings three cocktail dresses for me to try, and I choose a plum one. It's strapless and chiffon, and it flares at the waist, falling in waves to my knees. I pair it with a crystal necklace and earrings, leaving my hair down.

But the most important part of the outfit—the shoes—makes me happy. When Penny sent me the options, I ordered a pair of cranberry-colored Vans. If I had more time, I probably would have gotten crafty with them, adding jewels or something, like I did when we were in college. But alas, PLG ruined my week, so I'll need to settle for non-bedazzled sneakers. Still, it's a cool look, I think.

Hunter texts me when he's done with his game. I tell him he doesn't need to come and pick me up if it's inconvenient. The ball is being held right downtown, near City Hall, so it's a short Uber from my apartment. But he writes back, insisting I let him drive.

He also won't let me just run out to the car when he gets there. Instead, he double parks and walks all the way up to my apartment. When I open the door, I can't help smiling.

"It's fake dating, Hunt. You don't have to be this attentive," I say, but the words fade away as I take in the sight of him in a tuxedo.

Has Hunter always been this amazing looking? Probably because he looks the same as he always has—longish brown hair, glasses, and his ridiculously in-shape and gorgeous body. He leans against the doorway to my place, tucking one Converse-clad shoe in front of the other, and smiles, revealing the same dimple. He's the same, but tonight, the force of him hits me differently from how it has in the past.

I'm struck dumb staring at him, but he doesn't seem to notice. He checks out my dress and my shoes, and when he meets my eyes, there's pure admiration. "You look beautiful, pretty girl."

He has called me "pretty girl" lots of times, always when I take the time to get dressed up. Hunter has seen me at my grossest. We went to college together. He's seen me sloppy drunk, and he's seen me hungover. When I dated Nate, Hunter lived across the hall. He's watched me brush my teeth, and there's no way to look cute when brushing your teeth. "Pretty girl" was always his way of telling me he noticed when I tried to put myself together or took the time to get made up. It's really sweet, actually.

"Thank you." Am I blushing? "You look really sharp tonight, too, Bossy."

He pretends to swipe at a nonexistent bit of lint on his shoulder. "I mean, it's not sweatpants and a hoodie, but it'll do," he says, and I laugh, reaching for my black clutch that holds my phone and lipstick. When I turn back, he scowls. "Where's your coat, woman?"

"I don't have one that looks good with this dress." I point to the black pashmina I pulled out of the depths of my closet. "That's cashmere. It'll be fine."

"You're going to freeze." He glances around the room as if searching for something to cover me up. "It's cold tonight, Vi."

"I know, Hunt," I fire back. "But this is cashmere. It's warm. And you're driving me. I won't be outside much." When he continues to glower at me, I roll my eyes. "I promise I'll be fine."

He seems to debate that before he finally nods. I pick up my shawl and drape it over my shoulders. His brows furrow, and he closes the distance between us. When he stands this close, I need to look up at him. I'm not a short girl, but tonight, I don't have heels on. Even in heels, he's got a few inches on me. So tonight, he towers above me.

Again, I'm struck by how good he smells. Has he always smelled this good? It's something piney but citrusy too. Whatever it is, it's delicious.

I watch his face as he reaches for the pashmina. He pulls it tighter around me, and I can practically see him worrying about how cold I'll be. His concern fills me with affection. It's just like Hunter to worry about that.

But that isn't what catches me off guard. No, it's when his knuckle grazes my collarbone, and heat slices into my stomach. Even when he steps back to admire his work covering me up, the place where he touched me tingles with awareness.

He doesn't seem to notice, though. Instead, he nods. "That'll do, I guess. The venue has valet, so you're probably right."

To hide my reaction, I step back. "So I look okay, Boss?"

"You're perfect," he shoots back. This time, our eyes meet. The heat in his gaze surprises me, and it mixes with the awareness already zinging through me. I don't know what to say, so I can only stand there, looking up at him, trying to understand.

Something tentative covers his expression. "Vi?"

"Yeah?"

"I just wanted to..." He clears his throat. "Well, I wanted to make sure you were okay."

I'm not okay right now, not with this attraction swirling in my stomach. But surely, that's not what he means. "Okay?"

He inhales and squares his shoulders. "I felt like things were... strange after we danced last weekend."

"Strange?"

He nods. "And we were both busy this week. So I just wanted to make sure that everything was good. With you. With us."

Is it? "Of course. We're fine."

We are, too. At least, we're not un-fine. Just because I'm feeling some new and inconvenient attraction to my best friend, that doesn't mean things need to be weird, right? Sure, we need to go to a fancy ball and pretend to be dating, and if my stupid body keeps reacting to his like this, it's going to be a long night.

But I wave that away. "Everything is good. Just great."

He doesn't look convinced, but he nods anyway. Stepping aside, he motions me toward the door and then follows me out. He waits while I lock up, and then he places his hand at the base of my spine to escort me down the stairs.

I feel the warmth of it through my gown the entire walk down to the street together. He opens the door for me, and I slide into the warm Tahoe.

As he circles the back of the car, I give myself a pep talk. Hunter's attractive. I've known it objectively, but now my body seems to have figured it out. I inhale and breathe out slowly. This is fine. It doesn't mean that anything has to change. Hunter and I have been through so much together.

He slides in behind the wheel, and we head off. He's right—there's a valet right at the door, and the walk inside isn't too cold. That doesn't stop him from staying close by my side and watching me, probably scanning for any sign that I'll become hypothermic.

Inside, we're given a seating card, and we make our way to our assigned table. When we get there, June appears at my side and pulls me into a hug. "Violet. I was so happy when Duke said you'd be here."

I squeeze my friend back, and her presence makes me feel less confused about whatever is going on with Hunter. "I'm happy to see you, too. Has it only been a few weeks?" It feels like forever. *Thanks, PLG.* I hold her away from me and look her over. "How are you feeling?"

It's only been about a month since she donated a kidney to her foster mother. Between her surgery and moving in with Duke again, it's been an eventful fall. But she looks the picture of health.

She squeezes my fingers. "I'm great. Really."

I nod. From behind me, Hunter places his hand on my arm. The heat of it seeps into me. He motions toward the bar. "Did you want something?"

"A glass of champagne?" I hadn't been planning to drink, but that's not too strong.

He points to June. "Would you like something?"

She shakes her head. "Duke ran to get me something already. Thank you."

He nods and sets off, leaving us to get settled. I force myself not to stare at him as he makes his way across the ballroom to the bar.

"How is Duke?" I ask June to distract myself.

"Duke's great," she says with a smile, taking the seat next to me. "Better than great."

"I'm glad to hear that." It's the truth. No one deserves happiness more than June. But I can't help feeling a pang of envy. June found love with a man who adores her. Duke may be a little rough around the edges, but he's got a heart of gold. I want that, too, someday. Except every time I think about making space for it, I shy away from the thought.

"Actually," June says, dragging out the word. "I've been meaning to stop by. I left a message earlier this week."

I shake my head. "I'm so sorry. Work..." I trail off, though, as she drops her hand on the table in front of us. A huge diamond sparkles on her ring finger, bright in the chandelier light in the ballroom.

I point to it. "June? Is that...?"

She glances down before swiping a strand of her red hair off her face and flushing. "It is. It's an engagement ring. Duke asked me to marry him, and I said yes."

My heart swells for my friend, and I lean forward to fold her in another hug. "Oh, my God. That's amazing!" I can't stop grinning. "I'm so happy for you guys."

June returns the hug, and we both sway back and forth. "I know, right? I can't believe it. I didn't expect it at all, but it's everything I've ever wanted."

Pulling back, I give her a once-over. "Let me see that ring properly."

June extends her hand. The diamond is huge, glinting in the sun from the kitchen window. The ring really is beautiful. It's classic, a round solitaire in a four-prong setting. But a diamond like this doesn't need anything else. It's perfect the way it is.

"It's stunning," I tell her.

"Thank you." She admires it, her face a mask of bliss. "We've already picked out the wedding bands, too."

"You have?" That feels fast. "Duke isn't wasting time."

"There's no time to waste. We're getting married next week."

I blink at her. "I'm sorry?"

June nods, still beaming. "Yes, we're doing a small ceremony. We don't want to wait any longer, what with me living with him and Tabby." Tabby is Duke's seven-year-old daughter.

"That's just so fast!" Where I come from, weddings are huge ordeals, and they take months, even years, to plan. "We're going to need to find you a dress, then."

June's eyes light up. "Yes! I was hoping you would say that. I was thinking something simple, nothing too extravagant."

I nod. "We can go shopping together. Maybe tomorrow even? There's no time to waste. We'll find the perfect dress."

June claps her hands together. "Yes! Thank you so much. I don't know what I'd do without you." June came from the foster system, and she spent most of her teenage and college years working and surviving. I get the impression she had little time for friends. I'm glad we found each other. I've missed the tight-knit community of women I enjoyed in college and in my sorority.

I smile at her. "You don't have to worry about that. I'm always here for you, no matter what."

Over her head, I catch sight of Nate, and my smile fades. He looks polished in a tuxedo, his hair tamed. But while some of the other girls in the room probably will find him dashing, I don't feel anything for him. Not anymore.

Maybe that should surprise me, but it doesn't. What does surprise me is that my coworker, Olivia, follows behind him. He gives me and June a dashing smile. "Good evening. You ladies look lovely." He motions to Olivia. "Violet, you know Olivia. June, this is my date. Olivia, this is June, Duke York's girlfriend."

June smiles at Olivia, getting up to shake her hand. "Nice to meet you."

Olivia offers me a wave. But the look on her face is one of false apology. She knew I was coming to this, so why didn't she say something? The only reason I can figure is that she thinks I'll be upset that she's with Nate.

I had no illusions we were close. We work together, and we go to the bar for drinks afterward. She's not a person I would trust with a secret. Still, it feels sneaky that she didn't say anything. If she were a real friend, she would have reached out.

I couldn't care less about them dating, though. Objectively, they make a pretty couple, but as they sit at our table and get comfortable,

I can't think of anything I want to say to either of them, so I chat with June. We discuss her wedding plans and catch up. And when I see Hunter returning to the table, my chest loosens as if everything is better with him here.

But thoughts like that are dangerous.

Hunter

"NATE'S HERE, I GUESS." Duke leans against the gleaming bar beside me. The venue is posh, maybe one of the nicest rooms I've ever been in. It's classy but not flashy and is decorated in a winter theme. Everyone around us is fancy. This is definitely not my comfort zone.

"Yay." I accept Violet's champagne flute from the bartender. He hands me my beer, and I give him my card.

"Brought a date." The bartender points to Duke, and he says, "A glass of pinot noir and a Diet Coke."

I sip my beer and glance back at the table. When I see who Nate brought, I curse under my breath. "Fuck. That's Olivia." I'd recognize her anywhere. I've been avoiding her advances since the summer.

"You know his date?"

"Yeah. She works with Violet." It's a feat not to wrinkle my nose.

"And that's a bad thing?" Duke studies Olivia.

I consider and then shake my head. "Not bad that they work together. Olivia's a mean girl, I think. At least, the things Violet says about her lead me to believe that. And I don't like girls like that."

"Same." He pauses, watching the bartender pour his drinks. "Does Violet like her?"

I choose my words carefully. "She doesn't dislike her. But I wouldn't say they're friends."

He nods in understanding. "So, what's up with you and Nate?"

"Me and Nate? Nothing."

"Hunter, you get along with everyone. You're a silent son of a bitch, but you don't cause problems. Head down, do your job. It's one thing I like about you." He takes his drinks from the bartender and pays. He motions to the side, and we step away from the bar traffic. "But you don't like this guy."

I won't lie to him. "I don't."

"We heard you guys were friends at Chesterboro." Duke's brows furrow.

"We were." I incline my head. "Then we weren't."

"Spill it."

I sigh. "Nate and Violet dated in college. He broke up with her when he graduated. I thought he was a dick about it."

"And now you and Violet are together," he finishes for me.

"Yes." It's true, for the purposes of this conversation.

Duke's mouth firms. "I see."

"With respect, Captain, I don't know if you do." I don't even know what's going on.

"Anything left between Nate and Violet?" he asks. I prepare myself to tell him it isn't his business, and he must see that on my face because he lifts his shoulders in a shrug of innocence. "I only need to know if this is going to be a problem in our locker room."

"I don't know," I answer honestly.

Violet said there's nothing on her end, but that doesn't mean Nate feels the same. From the way he acted at the airport yesterday, it's clear that something bothers him.

One thing is for certain, though. "This won't have any effect on my play. I guarantee it," I say. There's no way Nate will ruin what's going well for me.

"That's what I need to hear. Whatever is going on, just make sure it stays out of my locker room. Do you understand?"

"Loud and clear. And I completely agree."

"Good." He leans closer and glances around. When he's sure no one else is watching us, he says only loud enough for me to hear, "Though I heard from Coach that you might not be with us for much longer."

I nod and swallow. If Coach brought Duke in on the trade rumors, they must be getting more tangible. "That's what he said."

"I'll be sad to see you go if that's what happens." He gives me a half smile. "I like you, Mason."

Grinning back, I toast him with my beer. "Same."

His gaze falls on our table, where Violet and June have their heads together, talking. "What about Violet?"

"I'm sorry?"

"What happens when you leave? Between you two."

I consider my response. There's what I want, what I hope, and what I think could be possible. There is no guarantee for any of that. "I don't know what happens."

He studies me for a long moment, and I wonder what he sees. "June and I are engaged."

"You are?" Both of us are holding drinks, but I put my beer down to slap my captain on the shoulder. "Congratulations. June is wonderful."

"She is." He has a besotted look on his face, which I find amusing. Duke might call me reserved, but he's not a touchy-feely guy either.

"When did this happen?"

"Over the Thanksgiving holiday. The wedding is next week." He offers me a half grin. "Hope you can come."

I laugh. That was the most straightforward wedding invite ever, exactly like the groom himself. "I wouldn't miss it."

He glances toward the table again. He seems to consider whether he wants to say more before he finally says, "June thinks highly of Violet. I don't know her well, but I trust June's take on people."

"She's the best."

He nods. "Then don't waste time if you care about her. Life is strange." He pauses, swallowing, and a hint of sorrow crosses his features. I remember he lost his first wife soon after Tabby was born. "Don't miss your shot."

"I'll try not to, Cap. Thanks." I clasp him on the shoulder and then pick up my drink, nudging my head toward our table. "I need to get over there. In case she needs reinforcements."

He nods, waving me ahead of him. We weave our way through the tables, and I do my best to keep my face impassive around Nate. Did Violet know he was bringing Olivia? From the straightness of her spine, I suspect not. If I ask whether she cares, she'll deny it. But that doesn't stop me from feeling jealous. They were together for almost a year. There's history there.

When I get to the table, I hand Violet her champagne, drop my hand to her shoulder, and give it a quick squeeze to reassure her. Leaning down, I whisper in her ear, "Are you okay?"

She stiffens, and when she looks up at me, her eyes are wide. "Absolutely." But when she nods, it's too fast. Almost awkward. She reaches for her champagne glass and downs half the contents. It seems like she needs liquid courage. For Nate?

I take a seat next to her. Across the table, Nate nibbles on Olivia's ear. This is going to be a long dinner.

Violet

Dinner at the Sneaker Ball is delicious. I got the chicken, and Hunter got the beef. We shared both, and I can't decide which I liked better. Luckily, Colt and his date arrive and sit next to Nate and Olivia. That means Hunter and I mostly talk with Duke and June, so the evening is enjoyable.

I have a few glasses of champagne, but I sip and stick to my decision to keep it together tonight. Dessert arrives—cheesecake and cannoli—and Hunter gives me most of his, so I'm feeling pretty happy by the time the dancing starts.

The band starts by playing traditional couple-dance music. A few of the older couples get up, and the dance floor fills with ballroom dancers. Even in sneakers, everyone looks glamorous, decked out in their formal attire.

"Let's go out," I say to Hunter. He exhales like he was waiting for me to ask. He rubs the back of his neck, stalling.

Next to him, June shakes her head vigorously at Duke. "Absolutely not," she says, waving her hands.

Duke smothers a grin. "Come on, Freckles. It's for charity."

"I'm being charitable when I say no one wants me to knock them over out there." She gives him a pleading look. "Come on. You know how uncoordinated I am."

He leans over and whispers something in her ear. I don't know what he told her, but it makes her blush and push a lock of hair off her forehead. Pressing away from the table, she stands. "It's your feet's funeral then," she tells him.

Chuckling, Duke rises, takes her hand, and leads her toward the dance floor.

"What do you say, Bossy?" I ask Hunter. "Should we join them?"

I expect him to argue, but he rises and takes my hand. Like when he put his hand on my shoulder before dinner, the contact singes through me. His smile is soft, and I want to get closer to him. My heart pounds as we head toward the dance floor.

The music is slow as he steps closer to me. Holding my eyes, he pulls me against him. As the front of my body connects with his, I inhale sharply. His hand finds the small of my back. He cradles the other hand in his and tucks our entwined fingers against his chest.

As we sway, I glance up at him. He watches everyone around us, making sure we don't run into anyone. I close my eyes and place my head on his shoulder, trusting that I'm safe in his arms.

It's here, cocooned by his scent, that I accept the truth—I want Hunter Mason. Have I always been attracted to him? I don't know. The past couple of years have been complicated for me. Or maybe I complicated them. But pretending I don't want him is impossible now.

Briefly, I consider whether there's any way to go back. Life would be so much simpler if I could. Do I want that? A scared part of me says it does.

But right now, my body is alive in a way it hasn't been in a long time. He places the hand he holds against his chest and folds his other arm around me. His fingers graze the sensitive skin in the center of my back. A shiver vibrates through me, and a mixture of excitement and heat and some weird foreign joy cuts into my stomach.

The music fades, and we stop. Reluctantly, I pull away. When I look up and meet his gaze, I see my own chaotic feelings reflected there. It makes me take a step back.

"Um..." I smooth my hair, pulling the mass of it over my shoulder and worrying the ends. "You know, I'm going to go get a drink. Do you need anything?" I step back farther, the need to retreat racing through me. "Can I meet you on the balcony? In a second?"

Hunter's arms fall to his sides, and his face closes. I know him well enough to recognize when he goes into hiding. Usually, he reserves that face for everyone else. He doesn't show most people his emotions, but I've always considered myself one of the lucky ones in his trust. I hate that he's wary of me now, almost as much as I hate being wary of myself.

I turn and force myself to walk to the bar. There's no line, so I step right up. "A glass of champagne." Then I shake my head. "Actually, could I have a vodka and Diet Coke, please?"

"On to the hard stuff." Nate appears next to me. I resist the urge to step away from him. Since he and Olivia headed to the dance floor before Hunter and me, I wonder if he followed me. "Could you get me a merlot and a seltzer water?" he asks the bartender. "Are you having fun, Vi?"

"I am." I don't look at him.

"Us too." He leans his back against the bar, glancing toward the table.

I follow his gaze. Olivia sits, her face in her phone. "What do you want, Nate?"

"I just wanted to tell you I'm happy for you."

I do my best not to roll my eyes. "Thanks."

"I'm serious," he says with a laugh. His expression is genuine. "When we were together, I know you said you saw us as forever, but I think we both know now that's not true."

"No?" I ask, lifting my brows, wondering where the hell he's going with this.

He waves his hand. "Please. You know how you were in college."

"Do I?" I'm torn between wanting to hear what he has to say and wanting to run from this conversation.

He laughs again. "A party girl and people pleaser. Trying to make everyone happy." He shakes his head, still grinning as his words hit me like bullets. "I never knew if you wanted me or just wanted the pretty life everyone else pictured for us." The bartender arrives with our drinks. Nate drops a few bucks into the tip jar and picks up his. "You're different now, though. I hope you're both happy."

The bartender shifts my drink across the bar to me, and I scramble to think of a response, but there's nothing in my head. Nate lifts the seltzer to me in a silent toast and then leaves me there alone.

Lights swirl around me in this glamorous space—the crystal chandeliers, the women in their beautiful gowns, and the men in their tuxes. The music fills the room, some upbeat song from the eighties. I'm sure the band is doing a great job with it, but I can't hear the words.

People pleaser, people pleaser...

It stings. Worse, it feels like I'm bleeding out, like everyone around me can see what's inside me, and it's grotesque. Because he isn't wrong. It would be easier if he were. I could be indignant. I could write off his words as sour grapes, just a guy who is butt hurt to find his ex dating someone new.

I do like to please people. Nothing makes me happier than seeing everyone else happy. There's nothing wrong with that, is there?

When we were dating, I was so sure that our relationship would make everyone happy. Me, my parents, and my group of friends. That was appealing. Oh, I fell for him, but my parents approved thoroughly. After all those years fighting to qualify my choices to them, this was finally something I got right. Our breakup made me question my and everyone else's judgment.

My eyes slide to the balcony door. Hunter is out there, waiting for me. He's my best friend. Always there for me, always believing in me. He understands me even when I don't understand myself. Ten minutes ago, I figured out that I wanted him. Should I trust my own feelings? And what if I'm wrong? The pain of losing Hunter's friendship would make my breakup with Nate look like a vacation. But I'm sure of what I feel. It just took me a little longer to figure it out.

Fucking Nate, interjecting his unwanted opinion. I straighten my spine. Maybe I am a consummate people pleaser, but I know what I want right now—Hunter.

Decided, I head for the balcony. At first, I don't see Hunter. He's tucked into the corner, leaning against the railing. When I spot him, I'm struck again by how good-looking he is. His hair falls over his forehead as he stares down at the street below us. He's relaxed, but nothing about his position hides the muscles under his tuxedo.

He must feel me approaching because he stands, rising to his full height. I'm in sneakers, so I don't have the benefit of any extra height tonight. Still, this will have to do.

I set my drink on a cocktail table nearby and walk right up to him. "Hunter?"

"Hey." A furrow wrinkles his forehead as he scans my face. "You okay?"

I might have chickened out if not for the concern in his expression. Squaring my shoulders, I say, "I want to kiss you."

His eyebrows disappear under the shaggy hair on his face. "You do?"

I nod. "I do."

Confusion clouds his eyes. "Is this part of the fake dating arrangement?"

I didn't even remember that until he mentioned it, but as soon as he offers the excuse, I grab it with both hands. "Exactly. If we were really dating, we would kiss, don't you think?"

He considers. "Kissing would definitely be part of a real dating scenario between us, yes." His eyelids are heavy, and a shiver slides along my skin.

I straighten my shoulders. "Right. So, what do you say?"

"What do I say?" The corner of his lips tilts up. There's the faintest hint of stubble on his cheeks. Between the grin and the five o'clock shadow, he looks like a pirate. The mischief in his eyes sets my heart beating faster. "Is this a negotiation?"

"Do we need to negotiate?" I place my hands on my hips.

He shows me his palms, his smile lazy. "I have no idea. This is your show, pretty girl."

"Okay, then." I look around. There are only a few couples outside. Though there are portable heaters positioned throughout the space, it's still pretty chilly. "Right here?"

Hunter shifts, and shadows cover his face. I don't like not being able to see his eyes. "Do you want to kiss me right here?"

I nod and step forward because if I don't do it now, I'll lose my nerve. He places his hands on my shoulders, and his warm fingers massage the tense muscles there. Despite the anxiety rushing through me, I feel myself tilting into him, like a flower leaning toward the sun.

He drops his head. When he speaks, his warm breath fans my cheek. "Show me what you're thinking, Vi."

His face is still too far above me, so I rise onto my tiptoes and curl my hands around his neck. It doesn't take much force to pull his mouth to mine. When our lips meet, it's like all the puzzles I've ever left unfinished find their missing pieces.

Hunter

Violet's kiss is tentative and so sweet it makes my chest ache. It takes all my strength to stay still when her lips touch mine. If I don't hold it together, I'm going to make a scene on this balcony.

I let her take the lead, and her lips play over mind. My pulse races in my ears, and I grip her waist, my fingers digging into the fabric. Her breath mingles with mine, and I want to swallow her up. But there are people everywhere, so I need to contain my reactions.

She holds my mouth against her for long moments, and every instinct in me screams to take over, to control the movement, to kiss her like I want to. Her kiss is vulnerable, though. She's anxious, overthinking. Maybe even second-guessing the decision to do this in the first place. I hate that.

When she proposed we kiss, I didn't see the harm. Hell, I've wanted to kiss her for longer than I can remember. If she thinks it's just part of our fake-dating arrangement, it's light and fun. Nothing serious. But this... this is the definition of serious. It takes everything in me to hold my shit together.

When she breaks contact, every nerve ending in my body is on fire. Her gaze meets mine, and I know immediately this is all wrong. Her expression is unguarded as her eyes search my face. The silence hangs thick between us, and then she sighs. When she swipes a strand of hair off her forehead, I want to pull her against me. I want to curl my body around hers and shield her from whatever is upsetting her, even if it's my fault. Especially if it is.

But this isn't the place. Damn it. I should have known I couldn't fake anything with Violet.

Before she can step away from me, I catch both of her hands in mine. She doesn't meet my gaze. "Violet." I wait until she makes eye contact. "Let's get out of here."

She nods and pulls her fingers from mine. I'm right on her heels, though, as she heads back into the ballroom and weaves through the other partygoers, making her way back to our table. June and Duke are the only ones there, and Violet gathers her bag. I don't hear what she says when she leans next to June's ear, but they hug. Violet wraps her scarf thing around her.

I hold out my hand, and I can tell she's wary. Finally, she slides her fingers into mine. I squeeze them and lead the way toward the exit. In the corner of my eyes, I see Nate and Olivia, their heads together. Taking a step to the side, I steer us away from them. Run-ins with him won't help anything.

I already have the valet tag out of my pocket when we get to the lobby. There's no one else waiting, so the guy heads right off to get my Tahoe. Violet tugs her wrap around her, and once again, I doubt it's warm enough for her. I debate pulling her against me, but I'm so tuned up already I don't even trust myself with innocent contact.

The valet arrives with my car, and I walk Violet around, helping her up. She's still not looking at me, and I grit my teeth as I head back and slide behind the wheel.

The radio is on, and neither of us changes the channel. The ride to her apartment is only a few blocks, but it feels much longer with the silence between us.

I get lucky, and there's a parking spot at the end of her block. It's not that big, but I maneuver my SUV into it. Maybe I'm off by a few inches, but this is Philadelphia. They'll give me a second.

"You don't have to walk me..." She stops when I give her a look. "Right." She sighs again, like the sigh she offered on the balcony. She's out the door before I can say anything.

I'm screwing this up.

"Fuck," I mutter to the silent car.

Then I reach for my handle and hustle out after her. Jogging, I catch up to her at the door. She fumbles with her key, so I cover her fingers and take it from her. With quick work, I let us in, and we head up the stairs to the second floor.

I search my brain for something smart to say. A way to apologize for whatever happened back there. The problem is, I don't know how to explain it. How do I say that if I had really kissed her back, really let myself go, that I would have made things inappropriate?

She pauses on the landing outside her door and holds up her hand. "Hunter. I'm sorry." She meets my eyes. "Fake dating was my idea, and it's been my idea to keep it going. I shouldn't have pushed the kiss. It's not what you wanted."

I blink at her, then glance behind us. There's no one on the stairs, and I don't think there's going to be. Violet's apartment is one of three in this building, each apartment taking its own floor. I don't think I've ever seen the other occupants.

Inhaling, I step closer to her. There's only an inch or two between her and her door. It's still locked, though. The position makes her need to look up at me. "Violet?"

Her eyes blow wide, and all the lust I stoppered on the balcony comes roaring to the surface. "Yes?"

"Is that what you think? That I didn't want to kiss you?" My voice is barely a whisper.

She swallows, scanning my face. "Well, you agreed to it."

"I definitely did."

"But, well, you didn't... I mean, it just didn't seem like you..." She furrows her brows, tries again. "You didn't..."

"I didn't kiss you back very well."

She purses her lips. "No. You didn't."

I've always wondered if there would be a moment between us, a time when it would become clear that I either needed to step forward or backward with her. Maybe there wouldn't have been... except for that kiss. Now we're here. Either I tell her the truth and take a chance, or I lie and hope that everything can go back to the way it's always been.

I don't want everything to go back to the way it was. "I'm the one who should be sorry, Violet."

"Why?"

"Because I thought I could kiss you and pretend I didn't feel anything."

Confusion lines her face. "I don't understand."

I guess I need to spell it out. "I've wanted to kiss you for a long time. Way before fake dating. Probably years."

"You have?" Her voice is a whisper.

I nod. "Yes."

"Why haven't you?" she asks so softly I can barely hear her.

"You didn't want me to." I won't soften the truth. I've always known where I stood with Violet.

"You're right. I didn't." The words sting, but they're not unexpected. I'm glad she didn't pretend.

I swallow hard. "That's why I haven't."

She inhales. Her eyes meet mine, and she's not tentative right now. "But tonight, I did."

"You did?"

She nods. "Yes."

"What about now, Vi?" I step closer, closing the space between us. Her head tilts back farther as she looks up at me. "Do you want me to kiss you now?"

I hold my breath, unsure what she'll say. Certainty shines in her eyes, and she nods again. "I do. Show me what you're thinking."

I don't need to be asked twice. I close the distance between us, pressing my body against hers. My hands cup her face, and I allow my fingers to slide around her nape. Then I take her lips with a groan.

While she controlled our balcony kiss, this is all mine. Her mouth opens on a gasp, and I slide my tongue between her lips. She tilts her head to accommodate me, and I make sure my fingers are between her and the door, cradling her.

There's nothing shy about the way I kiss her, and there's nothing tentative about the way she responds. This kiss is a possession, a claiming, and Violet meets me in the middle of it. Her fingers grip the front of my shirt, pulling me closer to her, and her lips move with mine. There's nothing vulnerable here, only lips and tongues and teeth.

It's magic. I want to touch her skin, breathe her in. I want to slide my hands down her back, cup her ass, and pull her more firmly against me. She can probably feel how much I want her, even now. We're close but not close enough. There's no way to get us close enough here, though, on the landing in front of her apartment door.

That thought sobers me. I pull back, my blood still pounding in my ears. This isn't a public place, but it's not private. This isn't the time, either.

Her breathing isn't steady, and hearing it fills me with possessive satisfaction. Her hair is messy where I tangled my fingers in it, so I smooth it away from her face as best I can. "There isn't a day that goes by when I don't want to kiss you. But I'll never kiss you—not before and not now—unless you ask me."

"Hunter..." She wraps her arms around herself.

This was too much, probably too fast. I feared that would be the case, but I hoped I was wrong. "Nothing has changed, Vi. Not for me. We can be whatever you need us to be, just friends or otherwise."

Just because she's overwhelmed right now doesn't mean that she's out of the game. She just needs some time to think and process. I can give her that. She can have all the time she needs.

"I think I need to go in," she says. Squelching my disappointment, I nod.

I retreat to the top of the stairs, and she puts her key in the doorknob, turning. I cast around for some way to leave this that isn't so heavy. "Duke and June's wedding is on Thursday night. I'll drive us?" I stop myself from saying that we'll go together. The more casual this feels, the better right now.

Her door opens, and she nods. "Sure. That sounds great." Stepping through the door, she waves. "Good night, Hunter."

"Good night, Violet." I wait until she closes the door behind her and engages the lock. Then I head down the stairs. I can't help wondering if I blew everything.

Violet

AFTER I LOCK UP behind me, I don't go inside any farther. My legs refuse to carry me. In Penny's beautiful plum cocktail dress, I fall against the door and close my eyes right there in my entryway.

Every nerve in my body still vibrates, and I can feel Hunter's lips as if they're still on me. I press my fingertips against my mouth, hoping the contact will make me feel more in control of my racing emotions. It doesn't work.

On the balcony, Hunter was distant. The kiss was pleasant, but I felt like he wasn't into it. I could have been kissing anyone. When it was over and he asked to leave, I knew I'd messed up. The entire ride home, I berated myself. I shouldn't have asked him for that kiss. Desperately, I tried to think of ways to apologize, things to say that would repair the damage I'd done. I couldn't come up with anything, and the longer I waited to say something, the worse it got. By the time we hit my front door, I was miserable. I would have said anything if I could keep my best friend—that it was a horrible mistake and that I never should have taken chances with our friendship that way. I don't know if I believe any of that, but I would have said it.

But then his kiss... holy shit. I've never been kissed like that before. Hunter kissed me like I was the last sip of water available in a desert.

He held me as if letting me go wasn't even an option. More than that, he held me as if I didn't have to hold myself up. I could have leaned into him and let go. He would have caught me.

Shivering, I wrap my arms around myself. The feel of his mouth against mine was an awakening. I don't know what I expected, but I definitely never expected fire.

But now that I know that it's combustion when our mouths touch, how am I ever going to look at him again without thinking about that—how it felt to have his hands grip my head, his thumbs on my cheeks, and his mouth on mine? Even if I could forget, would I want to?

I press my palm against my forehead, shaking my head. I don't know the answer to any of those questions. How could he think nothing had changed? I don't know exactly what happened, but that wasn't "nothing."

Shaking my head, I get up and kick off my sneakers. What I need is a long shower, a snack, and my bed. But after I manage those things, I find myself awake late into the night, the replay of that kiss in my mind chasing away my sleep.

I'm saved from seeing Hunter right away. He leaves for a couple of away games on Sunday. To distract myself, I go into the office to get caught up on administrative tasks I let go last week while we were finishing our PLG project. My desk is in order by the time I head home at dinnertime.

Though I don't sleep well, I feel confident about starting the week Monday morning. I always love the thrill of a new project. Considering I received the highest marks for my performance at PLG, I expect I'll get reassigned quickly.

I've barely put down my tote when Caitlyn, my supervisor, appears next to my desk. "Good morning. I was wondering if we could have a quick chat."

"Sure." I snag my travel mug off my desk and follow her.

In her office, she motions to the chair in front of her desk. "Have a seat."

She smiles at me and settles into the chair behind her desk. I don't know that I've ever seen her desk this tidy. She must have spent part of the weekend getting caught up as well.

"First, I wanted to compliment you on a job well done with PLG. I know that was a hard project, but you really rose to the challenge."

"Thank you. To be honest, I really enjoyed working on that. Especially with Sepana. She's a real rock star in London." I embellish a bit because I wouldn't really say I enjoyed the project, but I can't deny I'm satisfied with the way everything turned out.

"It's funny you say that, because I received similar feedback about you from the London office." She places her palms down on her tidy desk and gives me a winning smile. "In fact, they have approached me about extending your contract with them."

"Extending my contract? Don't you mean everyone's contract?" This project required seven contracted analysts.

She shakes her head. "Not at all. They've only asked for you."

"I don't understand. Why only me?" The parameters of our work were pretty straightforward. It required a lot of long hours, but we completed all the objectives that were originally set out.

"It wouldn't be about any of the things you've already worked on. They wanted to bring you on to help in the performance-reporting department." She shuffles some papers on her desk and slides a small stack across to me. "They would like you to help both with the coding and the financial aspects."

I scan the paperwork in front of me, focusing on the primary object in the job description. "This seems like they want me to help build out their platform."

She smiles. "Exactly. That's exactly what they want you to do."

I grind my teeth to keep from commenting. Last week, I made the mistake of complaining to Sepana that their performance platform is too rigid and doesn't offer as many customizations as it needs to. Apparently, I got myself into something.

"They're offering you a raise. Fifteen dollars more an hour." She makes this announcement like I should be thrilled, and maybe I should. It's never wise to scoff at more money. But if I work with PLG on their performance platform, I won't be able to continue with my programming on my dessert project—the thing I've been working on at home for the past few months. I'll be unable to sell it because I'm sure that PLG will make me sign another non-compete clause. They did that with the last project. That would tie me up and keep me from doing anything with my private work for an unspecified amount of time. But I can't exactly tell Caitlyn that. She doesn't know I've been programming on the side.

So instead, I smile even though it feels forced. "That's wonderful."

"We won't have all the details of the new agreement until after Christmas. I see that you have requested paid time off next week, during the holidays. That shouldn't be a problem. Take the week. By the time you come home after the new year, we should have a new arrangement hammered out for you." She pulls the paperwork back toward her, and I can see that she's pleased. They probably complimented her on my good work, too, and gave her some kind of bonus. I'm happy for her even if this complicates my plans. "There are a few ad hoc jobs that should carry us through this week. I've emailed you the specifics."

I stand and nod. "Sounds good."

She doesn't respond, but I'm sure she has dismissed me.

At my desk, I scan my inbox, but my mind strays to the ramifications of this new project. I don't know what I hoped to do with the work I've been doing at home, but I never expected to use it like this. I'm sure that she thinks that a fifteen-dollar-an-hour raise is a big deal, and maybe it is. But if they are giving me fifteen, that means they're receiving much more for my work. I'm not sure how I feel about that.

My phone rings, and I answer it. Within minutes, I'm tossed into the flow of my workday, but I can't shake the nagging feeling that this isn't the right path for me.

Hunter

Violet is avoiding me. I've been out of town since Sunday, at games in Illinois and Ohio, so I haven't been able to do much more than text. Her responses don't sound normal. It's not that they're short. I mean, they are, so that might be some of the problem. But my biggest issue is they're impersonal. She doesn't ask questions about the games. I send her pictures from the airport and the hotel, just like I always do—things that I think she'll find funny or interesting. But she's not responding the way I expect her to.

I want to blame it on work, but she just finished her project last week. I expected this week would be lighter, especially because it's the week before the holidays. No matter what the cause is, I refuse to let this go on too long. Which explains why I stand outside of her apartment on Wednesday night with a bag of takeout and a bottle of wine, pressing the buzzer for her intercom.

Her voice carries over the speaker. "Hello?"

It's a relief to hear her voice. "Hey. It's me. Can I come up?"

There's a pause, and then she buzzes, letting me in.

I skip up the stairs to her landing, and as I wait for her to open the door, I can't help but replay our kiss from the other night in this exact spot. My body hardens, and I try to shake it off. That's not what I should think about right now.

The door swings open, revealing Violet in what I like to call her staying-in outfit: joggers and an oversized sweatshirt. Her hair is on top of her head in a messy bun that she somehow makes look amazing. My fingers itch to touch her, but I give her my friendliest smile.

"I come bearing gifts." I lift the bag of Italian food I picked up on my way. "And this one"—I shake the bottle of wine—"is your favorite."

She steps back and grins. "You don't need to come with gifts, you know. In fact, you never need an excuse to see me."

"Says the girl barely answering my texts." No reason to tiptoe around the issue.

She scowls at me. "I've answered your texts."

She's not wrong, but things aren't right either. "You're avoiding me."

She shrugs. "Fine. Maybe you're right. I might be avoiding you a little." She holds her finger and thumb apart a fraction of an inch. Then she takes the bottle of wine from me before heading into the kitchen. She sets it down and reaches for the wine opener.

"Well, that's a no-go for me," I say.

There are dark smudges under her eyes as if she hasn't been sleeping well. Concern floods over me, but I do my best to keep it off my face. Violet gets irritated when I point out how much I worry when she's not sleeping well. I know better than to suggest medications or supplements. She hates them all, saying they make her feel worse afterward.

I cross my arms over my chest. "So, what's going on in your head, pretty girl?"

She doesn't answer immediately, turning to the cabinets to retrieve a glass and a couple of plates. She glances back and asks, "Did you want a glass?" I shake my head. She brings the dishes back to the island and inhales. "Just a lot of stuff going on is all."

That's not the response I get. That's the response she gives other people, especially when she wants to pretend she's got everything under control. Usually, with me, she leaves all that bullshit at the door. I tamp down a flare of panic.

"Anything you want to share with me?" I ask. Because if something's going on between us, we need to get this out in the open immediately.

Over the past few days, I concluded nothing was going to come between us and our friendship. Maybe she's right and we never should have stepped over that line. The possibility that I lost our closeness has filled my gut with dread all week. So whatever we need to do to get back to being close, that's what I'm going to do.

"Well, work, for one." She pops the cork out of the bottle and pours a glass. "They want to extend me on PLG."

"That's good, though, right?" Having more work when you're a contracted analyst seems like it would be a good thing.

She shrugs. "Yes and no." She leans forward on her elbows. "Do you know the program I've been working on?"

We've talked about her coding and programming love before. She's always tinkering, but recently she's been working on something to do with finance that was inspired by her work at PLG. But I know little about programming, so most of it is another language for me. "Kind of."

"I've been working on a customizable program for businesses to track their performance and reporting." She pauses to see if I understand. I shake my head. "Big banks and investment companies can use more streamlined software. It's the specialized corporations that need individualization. PLG isn't as big, and they need something with more options, so that when their portfolio changes, they can adjust it without complete chaos. My program would work for people who have a lot of highly diversified assets." I nod to show her I understand. "Well, I made the mistake of mentioning it to a girl at PLG. She must have brought it up with her superiors because now they want me to come on and help them develop their platform."

"That's amazing," I say. Violet is brilliant, and I love it when others appreciate her talent.

She grimaces. "I guess. But that wasn't how I planned to use it."

"How were you planning to use it?"

She raises her hands and shrugs again. "I don't exactly know. Hadn't really gotten that far. I guess I kind of always thought I would build it out myself. Maybe talk with investors, then try to sell it to a big company on my own..." She shakes her head. "Like I said, I don't know exactly. But this wasn't part of my plan."

I hum quietly to let her know I'm listening, but I don't have a solution for her. "That's rough. What do you think you're going to do?"

"I'm not sure yet. But my boss and the Kellerman management want me to sign a new contract in January." The smile she gives me is tired, but it's genuine. "I got a raise, though. So cheers to that." She lifts her glass and takes another sip before setting it down and reaching for the takeout boxes. "Anyway. Are you hungry?"

This isn't right. Usually, I would get the stream-of-consciousness thought ramble. She would include every emotion, dissect it from every angle, and ask my take.

I catch her hand, and she meets my gaze. "Vi?"

"Yeah?" Her voice is breathy.

"Is everything okay? With us?" I need to know where we stand. I need to know if I fucked everything up with us.

She exhales. "I think so."

I analyze her face. She doesn't look cautious or guarded, just worn out. She doesn't look away, either. I decide to take her at her word. I don't really have a choice.

Dropping her hand, I reach for something casual, something like the old us. I rub my palms together. "I'm starving."

Luckily, the tension breaks. We eat together. The conversation is even like BK—before kissing. Part of me is relieved, and part of me feels a gaping loss. I try to ignore that. When we're done, I help with the dishes. To stretch out the evening, I suggest we watch a movie. It's not an unusual request. At least once a week, we hang out in her living room, watching something.

After a pause, she says, "Only if I pick.."

We settle into our usual spots—she in the couch's corner and I'm in the recliner. She drags her favorite fleece blanket over her, the one with the flying pigs wearing capes, and tucks her hands under her head on a pillow. I kick my shoes off next to the chair and stretch out. The movie she picks—standard romantic-comedy stuff—is nothing I would have chosen, but that's fine. We fall into a comfortable silence. I'm thankful for it.

When I look over halfway through the show, Violet's eyes are closed, and she's breathing softly. This isn't an unusual occurrence either. Violet struggles to sleep when left alone, but given a movie and my company, she doesn't have any problems. But I'm glad to see her sleep. Even with her eyes closed and her face soft, I can make out the circles under her eyes. So I don't wake her, and I stay in my seat until the end of the movie.

It's late when it finishes, so I quietly put on my shoes and sneak out, locking the doorknob behind me. On the landing, I check it to make sure it's latched.

I head downstairs and out onto the sidewalk for the short walk home, immediately regretting not bringing a jacket with me. A cold front arrived earlier this week, but they're calling for snow over the weekend. I love snow, so usually I would welcome a Bing Crosby-esque white Christmas, but we're supposed to go to Chesterboro on Saturday evening after my game. Hannah Marshall and Cord Spellman's wedding is scheduled for Sunday, Christmas Eve. I'm hoping the weather doesn't complicate our travel plans.

Maybe everything will be okay with Violet. Tonight felt almost normal. I meant what I told her the other night. She knows how I feel, and it's pretty obvious she's not interested in more. But I'd rather have this with her than nothing. She's too important to lose from my life.

Violet

Being near Hunter Mason is going to make me insane. Wednesday night, when he came to visit me, I was sure I had things under control. We ate dinner and chatted like everything was the same—like he hadn't given me the hottest kiss of my life on the landing outside my door.

But when he picks me up for June and Duke's wedding, I realize I must have just been bone tired. I fell asleep on the couch five minutes into the movie, after all. That should have been a sign. Still, I'm unprepared for the sight of him in a sports jacket, his hair still wet from the shower and slicked back to dry. He smells divine. I have no idea why I never noticed how good his cologne is, but I get the full force of it in the car. And the way he casually leans over to open the door for me? Fuck, that shouldn't be so hot.

It's a short drive over the bridge out of the city, and I do my best to make small talk. He goes along with it, probably because he wants to ease the lingering weirdness between us. We arrive at the restaurant in Haddonfield that they've rented for the ceremony and reception, and he parks on a side street. When he meets me on the sidewalk, he offers me an arm to help me walk on my heels. A part of me—the part who thought everything could go back to normal—dies.

Because there's no going back now. I've told myself that there could be an escape hatch, a way to return to the days before I wanted him with the fire of the sun. There isn't. I just don't know what to do about that now.

Hunter is a gentleman. He's completely platonic—exactly how things were before. He's got more practice at this than I do. If he was honest the other night—and there's no reason to believe he wasn't—he's felt more than friendship for me for a long time. This means there's a chance he's felt the way I feel right now for years.

How did I not see it? It all seems so obvious now. It's almost embarrassing.

He escorts me inside the restaurant like he's guarding royalty. The ceremony is small and lovely. June looks gorgeous in a pale ivory gown with long lace sleeves. Her red hair is arranged on her head in soft ringlets, and her eyes shine. Duke looks handsome as well, but he's as reserved as always. I don't miss the softness on his face when he looks at his bride, though, and it melts my heart.

Duke's daughter, Tabby, is here, and she makes the sweetest toast to her father and June before dinner, lifting a glass of soda high. As the night continues and a string quartet plays, I notice that Tabby's grandmother takes her home.

Afterward, on our ride back into Philadelphia, I watch the city go by, a blur of lights and traffic. June and Duke don't have a traditional family. June was a foster kid, left behind by an addict and raised by a lovely foster mother nearby. Any family Duke has is still in Canada, but he's close with his mother-in-law, who helps care for Tabby. It's a hodgepodge of love, and I'm so happy they've found it.

Hunter double parks in front of my place, and I don't even bother arguing with him about walking me up. He's going to do it either way. On my landing, he waits while I unlock the door. "I'll see you Saturday after my game?"

"I'll be ready." Sunday, Christmas Eve, is the day of Hannah and Cord's wedding. We will leave for it on Saturday night. He waves and leaves. I go inside like I don't want him to stay.

I take off on Friday. I already have off all next week, but the ad hoc work Caitlyn gave me is tedious. No reason for me to do it when someone else can. I had my hair cut and colored earlier this week—thanks, slow work week. So I spend Friday having my nails done and getting a wax, and I even treat myself to a massage. Part of me hopes it'll distract me from whatever is going on with Hunter. No such luck.

Saturday morning, the air gets a familiar chill. I didn't know the chill when I lived in Texas, but now, after living in the northeast for five years, I recognize it means snow is coming. Sure enough, the local news is beside themselves talking about the paths the storm could take. It impresses me that weather people in the northeast still get wound up about snowstorms. You'd think they would have it figured it out by now.

I watch Hunter's Saturday game on television. They win, and he shows up at my door about an hour later. When he pushes the intercom buzzer, I tell him through the speaker, "I'll be right down."

"Do you need any help?"

"No, I've got it." Some people might think I am a diva, but I know how to pack light. I've been traveling to Texas and back for years.

I lug my carry-on down the stairs and out onto the street. A dusting of snow already covers the sidewalks. If it's cold enough that the snow isn't melting, that doesn't bode well for the roads. Hunter gets out of his truck and takes my bag from me. He lofts it easily into the back seat. I wrinkly my nose. "Stupid snow. I hope we can get there before the worst of it hits later."

"Yeah," he replies, but I can tell he's anxious too. Chesterboro is only a couple of hours from here, but it's already dark. In the mountains, the weather can change within a matter of yards.

The roads are fine on the way out of the city. They're wet, but the highway crews are keeping up. There's a lot of holiday travel, so I'm sure they've been working overtime to prepare. But once we're out of the city proper, we head up the Northeast Extension and slow to a crawl. The snow is coming down heavily now, and I can barely see the cars in front of us.

We exit, and the road conditions worsen. The passing lanes are treacherous, but on the four-lane roads, one lane is well-maintained. We drive into rural areas, though, and it's clear that the local municipalities are struggling to keep up with the accumulation. I can't make out any of the lines on the roads. When we turn onto a stretch of two-lane road, I can see the strain on Hunter's face. His knuckles are white on the steering wheel. I turn off the radio so he can concentrate.

Someone pulls out in front of us, and we head into a long skid, barely avoiding them. Hunter's face is grim. "I think that's enough."

"I'm sorry?"

"Find somewhere for us to stay. I don't care what kind of hotel it is, but we need to get off this road."

"We have a hotel for the night already."

"We're not even halfway there yet, Violet. And we've been on the road for three hours." He casts a glance at me. "The storm is just getting worse. It's not safe for me to have you out here." His jaw tightens again. "Please find us somewhere to stay."

At first, I want to argue. But I'm a Texas girl—I don't drive in the snow. And honestly, I can't blame him for thinking it's too scary. I can't see the taillights of the car in front of us.

"You got it." With a few taps on my phone, I find what we're looking for. "At the next exit, a mile and a half up the road, there are a couple of hotels."

That last mile and a half takes forever, but we finally navigate the exit. At the intersection, there are two motels. One is the scariest-looking establishment I've ever seen. The other is a Budget Inn.

"Budget Inn or Bates Motel?" I ask.

Hunter barks out a laugh, and maybe it's all the strain of driving in the horrible weather and being stressed out, but we crack up. He pulls into the Budget Inn parking lot and maneuvers the Tahoe into an empty space. The place looks pretty full.

"Let's leave our bags here," he says. "I'll run back out and get them after we get checked in."

I nod and jump out into at least six inches of snow. The stuff is still coming down hard in big fluffy puffs. It's treacherous to drive in, but it sure is pretty. Around us, it coats everything, insulating the world. It's quiet and cozy. Like a painting.

We hurry into the lobby after stomping our boots on the mat. There's only one person in front of us at the registration desk. When we get to the frazzled clerk, Hunter says, "Hi, we'd like two rooms, please. Whatever you have is fine."

The girl behind the desk is already shaking her head. "I'm sorry. We're near capacity. The storm is bringing in a lot of travelers. We only have one room left." She taps on the keys of her computer. "And it's a smoking room."

I wrinkle my nose. "That's all?"

She nods. "I'm sorry."

"We'll take it," Hunter says with a sigh, already reaching for his wallet. "It's only one night. We just need somewhere to crash. Do you guys have a restaurant?"

She shakes her head, pointing to the hospitality corner. "Just that."

His smile is charming. "That'll do, I guess."

We get our key and hit up the snacks. They have a couple of Hot Pockets, and I grab some candy bars. We load up on water. The receptionist gives us a bag, and I head up to the room while Hunter goes out to get our luggage.

As soon as I swipe the card, I realize we're going to have a problem. I didn't ask if the room was a double or a single—I just assumed it would be two queens. She would have said if it was a single, right? But when the door swings open, there's only a king-sized bed in the center of the room, facing a television. There's a desk with a chair, and in the corner is a side chair.

I place all our snacks and drinks on the desk, turning to stare at the bed. A few months ago, the prospect of sharing a bed with Hunter would have been no big deal. We were friends. We could share a bed with no problem. But after that hot-ass kiss the other night and spending the past week doing my best to pretend I don't see him as more than a friend, everything is different.

I hear the swipe of the keycard in the door, and Hunter steps inside. His eyes widen when he sees me, and he doesn't even put our bags down. "What's wrong?"

Propping my hand on my hip, I point at the bed. "There's a bed."

His brow furrows. "They usually have those in hotel rooms."

I blow out an exasperated breath. "Hunter, there's only one bed. There are two of us."

He places the bags on the ground. "Okay…" He lets the word drag out.

"I mean, we need to share this one bed." Why is he being so thick?

"Yes. That's what I heard."

"You're not getting it." My voice is getting louder and higher pitched, probably because I'm starting to panic. "We, you and I, will need to sleep together in that bed. The two of us. Together."

"Right. That's fine, though. We've slept in the same bed before."

"No, we haven't!" I exclaim.

"Yes, we have." He lifts his eyebrows. "Remember, spring break?"

I press my palm against my forehead. He's right. When we were all on spring break in April, I was rooming with Penny, and she asked me to hang out somewhere else so she and Griff could have some time together. Since there were other couples all over, I ended up curling up to watch a movie with Hunter while Mikey Dischenski snored drunkenly in the other bed beside us. I fell asleep and crept back into my room in the morning hours.

"That doesn't count. Dizzy was in the bed next to us."

I can't believe he's this clueless. Suddenly, I'm angry. How dare he say he's wanted me for years one moment and then say he'll be fine the next? It's rude.

In a small, rational corner of my mind, I know I'm being silly. He's been a gentleman this week. Truthfully, he's always been a complete gentleman. He's thoughtful, concerned, and always watching over me. He's the calm in any of my storms. I shouldn't be surprised that he's not frazzled now.

He's never afraid of anything, unlike me. I'm afraid of everything. Is that what caused my disorientation this week? Is that why I'm freaking out now—because I'm scared? I shake my head. I'm not afraid of Hunter. But if I keep going like this—keep pushing him away or remaining on my guard with him—I'm going to lose him. It might not be now or this weekend, but it will happen. I'm not good at pretending. And with Hunter, I don't even want to try.

"Why doesn't that count?" He crosses his arms. "Spring break, I mean?"

I want to laugh and scream at him at the same time. But he already looks irritated with me. As always, his frustrated look is disarming. Any remaining second thoughts fade away.

My next words come out almost at a yell. "God, Hunter. Really? Because I'm hot for you. I wasn't hot for you then. But now I am." I prop my fists on my waist and glare at him, stepping closer. "I can't stop thinking about that kiss on the landing, and now every time we're together, I want to jump your fucking bones."

His eyes flare. "Do you, now?"

I laugh. "And you've been all, 'We can go back to the way things were before,'" I say, mimicking his voice. "But you know what? I can't. I don't want to anymore." Pointing to the bed, I stare up at him. "And if I lie on that bed next to you all night, and I can't touch you, I think I might just lose my mind."

His eyelids lower, and he closes the distance between us. The bravado seeps out of me, and I'm caught in the intensity of his stare. He reaches for my shoulders and draws me toward him until our bodies are flush with each other. One of his hands wraps around my waist, and the other buries itself in my hair. Helpless, I grip his waist, trying to hold on.

"We definitely can't have that," he whispers in my ear.

"Have what?" I say back softly.

"You don't get to lose it, pretty girl. Not without me." And then he meets my gaze, and I lean up and kiss him.

Hunter

As soon as her mouth meets mine, I'm lost. Her kiss is sweet, but the way I've wanted Violet isn't sweet.

I allow my hands to find her ass. She's got on those tight leggings that girls all seem to wear, and the spandex does amazing things to accentuate her backside. I lift her, and she wraps her legs around my waist. The new position gives her better access to my mouth, and I coax her on. The kiss deepens, and she threads her fingers in my hair. When she closes her fists, the bite as my hair pulls amps me up.

She's light in my arms, and I turn to sit, still kissing her. Settling her in my lap, I allow my fingers to find their way to the hem of her sweatshirt. I realize she's still in her parka, so even as the soft skin at her waist calls to me, I reach for the zipper. I don't break contact with her mouth, though. She doesn't want to stop kissing me either, it seems, because she barely gives me enough room to undo the zipper.

When she's free of the coat, I reach for her waist again and slide my hands under her sweatshirt and up her back. Fuck, she's so soft. With a quick flick, I unlatch her bra, smoothing my fingers along the skin there. She fumbles with the zipper on my jacket, so I take it off, letting it fall to the floor next to us.

My fingers find the bottom of her sweatshirt again, and I break off our kiss, dropping my forehead to hers. "Vi, I want to see you. Are you good with that?"

She nods. "Absolutely. One hundred percent. Amazingly good."

I chuckle, drop a kiss on her swollen lips, and then tug her sweatshirt up over her head. The bra I've already unhooked comes along, as well as her T-shirt. I don't get a moment to see her, though, because she reaches for my shirt. That won't do.

In a smooth motion, I pick her up again. The movement distracts her from trying to undress me, and she wraps her arms around my neck to hang on. "Hunter!"

"Hush. I got you." I carry her around the side of the bed. Holding her with one hand, I reach for the comforter and pull it down along with the top sheet. No way am I putting Violet's sweet skin on some nasty hotel comforter.

I place her on the sheets, and then I make quick work of my shirt, unbutton my jeans, and drop them. But I leave on my boxers because too much skin-to-skin will make this go too fast.

She tries to sit up, to reach for me, but I cup her cheek and kiss her. That stops her in her tracks. "Slow down, pretty. I've got you."

Something intense and unsure plays across her features. "Okay."

"You still want to do this, right?" I need to know we're still good to go.

"Yes. Definitely yes." She props herself up on her elbow to look at me.

I cup her cheek. "Great. Well, I've been dreaming about you for a long time. You'll have to excuse me if I want to take my time."

Her pupils get huge. "You've been dreaming of this?"

It's amazing to me she still has no idea how I feel about her. Right now, with her lying on the bed next to me, I want to tell her everything. I want to tell her I'm in love with her, that I have been for a long time. I want to tell her she's the most important person to me and that I want to be with her forever.

But I know she isn't ready for that. If I can't tell her yet, I can definitely show her. I lean in and kiss her again, but this time, I put everything into it. I smooth my hands over her shoulders, trying to calm her. Briefly, I press my fingers into the smooth muscles at the base of her neck, and her eyes close.

"Shift up," I tell her, and she does. I slide in behind her, guiding her to lie back against me. Her bare back meets my chest, and I groan. God, we haven't done anything yet, and I'm already more turned on than I've ever been.

She leans forward, and I smooth her long hair over her shoulder. She tries to look back at me, but I hush her again, and then I get to work on the muscles in her back.

At first, she tenses. I run my mouth along her skin, from neck to shoulder, and she tilts her head to give me better access. A very good sign.

I work on the tightest muscles at her neck first. She softens against me, so I keep going, remembering how tired and stressed she seemed this week. When she hums her approval, I feel like a superhero.

By the time I've tended to her back, her entire body is relaxed. I adjust her so that she's lying on me once again, and I can see the whole spread of her body. "Fuck, Violet, you're gorgeous."

Her golden hair is a waterfall around her shoulders. I follow the length of it to one of her perfectly peaked nipples. When I take it between my thumb and forefinger, her back bows up, and she reaches for my hand, covering it. She stretches her legs out, squeezing them together.

"Oh," she whispers.

I still. Her body has tensed up. "Did you want me to stop?"

She shakes her head emphatically. "No."

"So I should continue?" I ask. She leans back so she can see me, and I hold her gaze. She doesn't immediately remove her fingers from mine. "What's up?"

She glances at the lamp next to the bed. "Do you think we could turn that off?"

"Why?"

"It's bright."

"Yeah. So I can see you."

She turns. It's the smallest adjustment. "It's just... really bright." She almost sounds miserable.

I do a bit of a crab walk so I can see her face better. "Violet, I want to see you. Every curve of you is perfect for me. I know your face almost like I know my own. It's my favorite face. I've watched the curves of your body for years, underclothes." I kiss her lips, and she sighs. "I've imagined what you look like naked a million times. I want to see you because I'm sure the reality is better. But if you want the light off, we can do that. It's your call."

The uncertainty fades from her expression, replaced by desire. She shakes her head. "No. Let's leave it on."

I nod my approval. "Lie down and let me look at you."

She does what I ask, and I reach for the waist of her pants. Hiking up her hips, she helps me pull them down, and her panties come with them. She freezes for a moment. But after a quick glance at me, she exhales and settles.

"Good girl," I whisper in her ear. "That's right. I've got you."

She's splayed in front of me, lying between my outspread legs, and on display. Her breasts are full and perfect. I take one in each of my hands, testing their weight. So fucking soft. I run my thumbs over her tightened nipples, and she arches again into my touch, her breath a small pant.

My cock presses into the small of her back, almost painfully hard. I'm sure she feels it, and that drives my desire hotter. I slide my fingers down her sides, and the muscles in her belly jump, like she's intensely aware of every brush of my hands.

Leaning forward the slightest amount, I hitch under her knees and coax her thighs open so that the center of her is wide for me. I can see her easily because she's waxed, leaving only a small strip of hair on her lips.

I gently run my finger over them. "This is lovely."

She covers my hand again, and I pause. Her head twists and her eyes meet mine. There's heat there, so much heat. Her breathing is coming in soft gasps, and I can't help myself. I cover her lips, kissing her with all the fire I feel inside.

"Violet, I'm going to touch you now." I catch her fingers in mine and move her hand to the bed beside my hip. Then I do the same with the other hand. "I would appreciate it if you kept these hands to yourself while I learn my way around you."

Her eyes flare, and she nods. She's the picture of sex right now, her long blond hair falling around her shoulders, her breasts with their tight pink tips, and her legs spread wide for me. Unable to delay even another moment, I smooth my hands along the inside of her thighs and then slide my finger right along the folds of her.

She's so wet I have to close my eyes for a second to compose myself. Then I softly circle her clit, and she cries out. I allow my fingers to play across this softest place, learning her, reveling in the feel of her.

The need to taste her overwhelms me, so I shift to the side, guiding her to her back on the bed. She reaches for me, and I capture her hands, returning them to the bed beside her. "No, you don't. I need to see if you taste as perfect as you feel."

I situate myself between her thighs, hitching my arms under her so I can adjust her position. She looks down at me, her eyes heavy. She licks her lips, her chest rising and falling with her shallow breath.

I lick over her most sensitive skin. The taste of her could quickly become an obsession. Factor in being able to watch the bliss on her face, and it's addictive. My tongue plays over her soft folds. When her orgasm breaks, she cries out, and I help her ride out the waves of it, immediately wanting to see her like this again.

When she settles, I crawl up her body and curl her against me, pulling the blankets over us so she doesn't get cold. As her breathing steadies, I accept what I always suspected—I'll never get enough of this woman. I can only hope we have enough time for me to convince her this could be forever.

Violet

THAT ORGASM WAS A revelation. I'm no prude. I know how to get myself off, and I've orgasmed during sex plenty of times. Not all the time, but enough that I figured I knew what was what. Hunter proved to me I didn't know anything about it.

"If you knew you could play me like that, why didn't you ever say something?" I pant out to him, curling my face against his shoulder. "Not fair to keep that a secret."

I feel as well as hear his chuckle against my cheek. "Would you have wanted to hear that?"

I consider, but I don't really have to. No, I wouldn't have. Thinking about Hunter like that before hadn't felt safe. It terrified me, so I shied away from it. I can acknowledge that now, lying in his arms after an earth-shattering orgasm. I'm not ready to admit it to him, though, and I'm not ready to analyze the reasons. Right now, I want to just be here, at the moment.

When I don't respond, he presses a kiss on the top of my head and chuckles again. It's only then I realize he's still wearing his boxers, and he's as hard as a rock. I press into him, and the feel of him cradled in my belly sends heat racing through my body again. Part of me can't believe I'm already fired up again, but maybe it shouldn't be surprising.

"Hunter?" I whisper.

"Violet?" he whispers back.

"Please fuck me now?"

He barks out a laugh, and I grin along. I know Hunter better than I've known any of the men I've slept with—even Nate. All that should make this feel more serious or something. But it doesn't. Instead, it feels safe—somewhere I can laugh and let go.

"I'd love to fuck you now, Violet."

"Wonderful. Let's do that, then." I reach for the waistband of his boxers, and together we guide them down his legs. They end up on the floor with the rest of our clothes.

With a quick flip, he's got me on my back again. He straddles my hips, using his bulk to pin me into the mattress. His eyes are heated again, and he stares down at me. "Do your nipples taste as good as they look?"

I shiver. Once again, I'm surprised by how confident he is here. Maybe I shouldn't be. Hunter doesn't say much, but it's not because he's shy, and it's certainly not because he's submissive. He's always exuded quiet strength. Right now, it takes away all my uncertainty. I wouldn't dare feel self-conscious here, not when he's so sure.

"I honestly don't know what they taste like. I'm not that flexible." I roll my eyes at him.

"I need to find out, then." He leans forward, lapping one in his mouth.

Like before, when he touches me, it vibrates through my whole body. I buck up, pressing my breast into his mouth. Heat radiates through me, and I whimper, overwhelmed. I want to pull him closer and push him away at the same time.

He runs his tongue along the sensitive tip and then blows on it. The cold air is almost painful. “Settle, pretty girl. I’ve got you.”

As he moves to the other breast, I close my eyes and breathe. Because I believe him. He has me, and even though the feelings slicing through me are intense—almost painfully so—I know he won’t hurt me. That complete surety makes me let go and allow myself to feel the friction of his tongue. I lace my fingers in his hair, and he groans as I pull it softly. I shift beneath him, the pressure between my legs driving me. But he holds me still, curling his arms under my shoulders, cradling me while he drives me wild with his lips and tongue.

“Please, Hunter. Please,” I pant out. Between the pressure on my nipples and the friction I’m getting from rubbing my own thighs together, I’m near coming again.

“Please what, Violet?” he asks, his breath hot on my chest.

I tug his head up, meeting his eyes. “Please, come inside me.”

He must see how close I am because he pulls away. He’s gone for a minute, and I hear a wrapper. When he returns, he nudges my legs apart with one of his huge thighs. The feel of him pressing at my opening makes me wiggle and do my best to move him forward, coaxing him to come inside me. But he stills. Then he gathers my hands in his, and he presses them into the bed on each side of me, at shoulder height. The position, being held down, causes me to stop moving and meet his eyes.

“I said settle, pretty girl. You can let me,” he says, leaning forward to take my lips in his again. This kiss differs from our others. It’s not the possessive claiming most of his kisses are. This is a promise, and I melt against him, giving myself over to him.

I never thought I was the girl who would get off on submitting to someone else. Usually, during sex, I'm the instigator, the more dominant one. I know what I like, and I make sure I get it. Maybe it's because I've never trusted someone to take care of me before. But all Hunter has ever done is take care of me. Here, I'm sure he'll do that again. So I kiss him back, and he slowly presses inside me.

He's an unyielding force. He's big, and I feel the urge to shift, to ease his passage, but every time I want to adjust myself, he does it for me, surging and retreating at the slightest resistance, until he's seated deep inside me.

He pulls away from the kiss and leans back a little, with a furrow in his brow. His hands still press mine into the mattress, and I'm panting, staring up at him. He retreats, then presses forward again, watching my face. The third time he retreats, he leans back the slightest fraction, and when he pushes forward again, he hits some spot inside me that sends pure pleasure pulsing through me.

"Oh my God."

He smiles. "Violet, I want you to keep your hands here. Do you understand?" When I don't open my eyes, he pulls out and returns, hitting that spot again, making me moan. "Violet." He doesn't move, so I open my eyes and stare up at him. He lets my hands go, cupping my face. "Your hands. They stay here. Do you understand?" I nod. "Words, pretty girl. I need words."

"I understand." When he waits, I continue. "I'll leave my hands here." I press my fists into the bed next to my shoulders to prove I get it. Honestly, I'd do anything he asks right now if it means he'll keep going.

"Good girl." Then he grips my hips in his hands. "My pretty, good girl."

His praise sings through me, but I don't even get to dwell on that, because he's pulling out of me and pressing in again, hitting that spot that has me singing. When his thumb makes the softest caress on my clit, I close my eyes and let go of any illusion that I have any control right now. Because there's no way I would do anything that would stop the pleasure soaring through my body.

He continues, his rhythm steady and with feather-soft touches to my clit. But it's not hard enough or fast enough to send me over the edge. I can only swim in the emotions of it all, gasping and panting. I'm begging him now. "Please, Hunter. Please… I'm so close. It's so good… please, please…"

"Violet." His voice is harsh, full of gravel, and when I open my eyes, his face is a mask of control. "Tell me what you want."

"Please, Hunter." I'm barely forming cohesive thoughts right now, and he stops, buried deep inside me. When he presses against my clit, it's firm.

"I need to hear what you want," he demands, his eyes dark and intense. "Tell me what you want."

"Please, let me come." I practically sob the words. I don't dare move my hands, because he's proved he has control over my orgasm right now. So I tell him again. "Please, Hunter, make me come."

He leans forward to kiss me, and this kiss is a reward. "Absolutely, good girl." When he leans back, he finds that sensitive spot inside me at the same time his thumbs circle my clit, and this time, the pressure is perfection. His pace increases the slightest bit, and I explode around him, my inner muscles clenching him in an orgasm that's so powerful it's the perfect mixture of pain and pleasure.

I cry out, calling his name over and over as the waves take me. He keeps up his ministrations, making certain I ride out every second.

Then he grips my hips and plunges into me one more time, shouting his own release.

The calm afterward is absolute. He gathers me against him, and we curl up together, panting. Neither of us feels like talking, I guess. Hunter's breathing evens, and he doses off. I wrap him in my arms, inhaling his familiar smell.

Here, in the circle of his arms, I can't remember the reasons I didn't want to take a chance on this with him. Maybe they'll come back to me tomorrow. But right now, I allow myself to relax into him and just breathe.

Hunter

If I worried things would be weird between me and Violet, I shouldn't have. I wake up after she does, and she leans over and kisses me on the cheek. She's deliciously rumpled, and her smile is pure sex. "Good morning, handsome."

I grin. "Good morning, beautiful." I drag her closer, folding her against me. I curve my bulk around her, and she snuggles in.

She's warm, and I bury my face in her shoulder. The T-shirt she threw on with her panties to sleep in does nothing to hide her hard nipples, and they distract me. But as I reach for the hem to pay them proper attention, she swats my hand.

She points to her watch. "Text. From Shea. They moved the ceremony up to noon. We need to get going."

I groan. Foiled by a text. "What time is it?"

She's already squirming out of the covers. "Just after seven. But I don't know how the roads will be. We need to shower here."

"Showering, huh?" I wiggle my eyebrows at her. "That sounds like fun."

She giggles, slipping out from under the covers before I can reach for her again. I admire the view of her legs and backside as she heads toward her luggage.

After I use the restroom, I leave her to shower first. I've known her for a long time. She'll take longer than I will.

It takes a lot of self-control not to coax her into some shower play. But she's right—the roads. Violet doesn't drive in the snow. That's the original reason I offered to drive to Chesterboro months ago when we first found out Cord and Hannah were getting married here. After going to school here for four years, we're both aware it's rare to see the grass in December. We also need to find some food. So I behave while we get dressed. She insists on wearing heels, and I'm grateful the parking lot is mostly clear. But I still hold on to her tightly while we make our way to the car.

Luckily, the road crews seem to have caught up on the snow accumulation this morning. We stop and grab bagels when we see a sign. It's still slow going in spots, but we get into Chesterboro by eleven o'clock.

Violet's phone buzzes, and she frowns. "The country club doesn't have power. They're moving the ceremony to the hockey rink."

"Like, they're going to get married where the Chesterboro team plays?" There aren't any other sheets of ice in Chesterboro. The community uses the university's rink for lessons, and the high school hockey team uses it for practice and games.

"Yes. It has an emergency generator to keep the ice, so we'll have heat and power."

That makes sense to me. "I guess we'll head there, then."

We park, and the lot is full of cars and the Dazed Zealots' tour bus. That's right. Hannah and that band are good friends. Maybe we'll get lucky, and they'll play for us.

I help Violet inside, once again amazed at how she navigates even the worst weather in heels. It's a skill. I try not to glower at her dressy jacket. It doesn't seem heavy enough for how cold it is, but when I suggested she wear something warmer, she told me to zip it.

Inside, it's a college reunion, with lots of guys from Chesterboro, from the years Cord played there. Most of them play professionally now. Then there are a bunch of musicians and other performing artists. Hannah uses the stage name "Goldie," and her fame has exploded since the first time I saw her perform. It was at a dive bar outside of Chesterboro called the Pig's Tail.

The wedding planner ushers us inside, and sitting in the bleachers, I feel a sense of déjà vu. The ice here still smells the same. Violet and I grin at each other, caught up in the same nostalgia. We only graduated in the spring. It feels like both yesterday and forever ago.

The ceremony should feel thrown together, but it doesn't. The way Cord looks at Hannah... it's as if she's a pot of gold he found at the end of the rainbow and he can't believe his good fortune. Around us, there are more than a few tears, including Violet's. I squeeze her hand, and she gives me a watery smile. I am struck again by how gorgeous she is, how I never want to stop looking at her face. How her smiles make everything in my life better.

It strikes me that the way Cord looks at Hannah is probably the way I look at her. I love her, and I want our forever. Now that Violet and I have slept together, I wonder if she's thinking the same thing. Instinctively, I guess that it's too soon for her to know.

After last night, it's obvious to me we're as compatible in bed as we are everywhere else. In fact, it's better than I ever could have expected. The future feels like it's falling into place. As I continue to hold her hand, I allow myself to hope she'll see how right things are with us.

Violet

I HAVE NO IDEA how they pull off a classy reception at a college hockey facility, but somehow, they do. It must have taken a small army. The weather improves enough for the deejay to get here, and she sets up in the foyer. There are caterers scrambling everywhere, and they manage to pull off a beautiful buffet.

The reception begins. We already know that our evening flights out of Scranton are delayed. With no worries about driving anywhere tonight, everyone relaxes. For a makeshift wedding venue, the ice rink is pretty comfortable. There is an open bar and dancing in the foyer and team rooms, and it's wonderful to catch up with old friends.

Shea Carmichael, Colt's sister, has always been one of my favorite dancing buddies. Shea, Penny, Ivy, and I are out on the dance floor for so many songs that I lose count. When my feet hurt, I beg Shea to take a break, and we find a corner of the waiting area and have a seat.

"I haven't had a chance to tell you yet, but I'm so happy for you." She folds me in a hug. Shea is a little thing, just over five feet tall in high heels, but her hugs have always been huge. "When Penny told me you and Hunter had finally gotten together, I literally squealed."

That makes me laugh, and I shake my head, grinning. "I had no idea everybody was taking bets on us."

She lifts her shoulder. "Not really bets..." she hedges. "More like we were all hoping for you."

"I can't believe none of you said anything. Especially Penny. She's not exactly a vault of secrets."

"I don't think any of us wanted to do anything that would discourage you both." She squeezes my hand. "After everything happened between you and Nate, you were so skittish. We figured it could either go way. Either Hunter would get sick of waiting for you, or you would wise up."

"Thanks a lot," I tell her. But we laugh together.

"I'm teasing you. It's just that you two always seemed so happy together. The only time your sadness ever left was around Hunter. None of us could figure out how you didn't see the way his eyes lit up every time you walked in."

Is that true? I'm sure I don't know.

Shea's boyfriend, Linc, joins us. He sweeps her to her feet, and they head to the dance floor for a slow dance. I glance around. Hunter is talking to Declan Mitchell near the bar. Declan and his girlfriend, Ivy, apparently got engaged on the ride here. I'm certain Hunter is congratulating them.

I pull my phone out of the little clutch I brought with me and open my photos. I skim through them to last year when we were last in Chesterboro—pictures of sorority parties and post-hockey-game celebrations. The memories make me grin. But I pause on the ones where I'm with Hunter.

Usually, when I look at pictures, I'm checking my hair or makeup, seeing if my position shows off my legs or makes me look skinny or some other nonsense. But now I search for signs that Shea's right.

In some of the pictures, I can see my sadness. I don't know if it would be noticeable to everyone, but I know myself. I recognize it for what it is. But the times that I look happiest are when I'm with Hunter. Other people come and go in the pictures. Groups of our friends join us, but the constant is him.

I allow my phone to drop into my lap. I liked it better when Hunter was around, but I attributed that to friendship and understanding. How did I not see what everyone else seemed to understand?

Across the room, Hunter shifts, his eyes searching, and I know he's looking for me. I get it. I do the same thing. I don't know what's going to happen now. But whatever Hunter and I have, it started with friendship, and maybe that's the difference. Maybe this time, I'll get it right.

Hunter

I PLANNED TO FLY to Missouri to visit my parents after the wedding, and Violet was supposed to travel to her parents' home in Austin. But most of the flights out of Scranton are delayed, so we spend Christmas Eve together in a hotel room outside Chesterboro, Pennsylvania. Objectively, this room is nicer than the one we stayed in last night. Fortunately, the electricity is back up in the area, so the hotel can serve dinner.

Not that we make it to the restaurant to eat. The second we get into our room, we're reaching for buttons and zippers. When our bare skin finally touches, both of us sigh. It's gratifying to see that she's as desperate for me as I am for her.

This time, when we make love, it's with less finesse and more frenzy than last night. I'm starved for her, desperate to get as close as possible. This trip is like a mini honeymoon, and I don't want to waste any precious moments I have. We fall to the sheets in a tangle of reaching hands and seeking mouths. When we come together, I want to imprint myself on her, to touch her soul in the way she touches mine.

In the morning, she'll be in Texas, and I'll be in Missouri. I only have Christmas Day with my family, and then I'll need to be in Colorado for a game. I won't see her again until the weekend, for her parents' New Year's Eve party. A week feels like a long time. What's between us is so new, and it feels fragile.

In the aftermath, I listen to her heartbeat, and our breathing syncs. Maybe it's because it's Christmas, but I'm feeling thankful, and I want to stay like this forever.

But hunger calls. We order room service and eat it picnic-style in our room. After that, we spend some quality time in the shower, and I nearly drown myself in pleasing her.

When we're out, there's a knock on the door. I don't know if it's Hannah's doing or if the hotel is feeling festive, but we get a room service delivery for dessert later, complete with candles and a bottle of champagne. Violet and I curl up on the bed, and we share chocolate-covered strawberries and tiramisu.

She lifts a glass of champagne. "To the good life." She's already had a couple of glasses as well as whatever she drank at the wedding, so her cheeks are pink, and her eyes are bright. "Room service and the hottest man I've ever met."

I chuckle, clinking my glass against hers. We sip, and I reach for her. "You're too far away."

She comes into my arms willingly, and we curl together. We left the lights off, using the candles instead, and I opened the curtains. Outside, the moon lights up the snow-covered world.

Violet sighs at me. "I don't want to go to Austin tomorrow. I want to stay right here."

I tighten my arms around her, understanding exactly how she feels. "I know. But the Tyrants won't like it if I don't show up for work on Tuesday," I say, and she laughs. "Besides, my parents are expecting me tomorrow." I wish she were coming with me to Missouri instead of us separating.

"I know. I don't want this to end."

"Me neither." I kiss her forehead. "But I'll see you on Saturday after my game, and we'll go to your parents' New Year's party together. Oh, do I need anything special to wear?"

She wrinkles her nose. "It's black tie."

Of course, it is. "I'll be prepared."

We spend the rest of the evening talking and laughing, enjoying each other's company while we can. But both of our flights are early the next morning, so eventually we snuggle together under the covers and drift off.

The moonlight outside the window has barely faded when we wake up to catch our flights. Violet hides her face under the covers, grumbling when I poke her, which makes me grin. I wish I could take her with me to Missouri, but she needs to see her family the same as I need to see mine.

I sit up and stretch, trying to shake off sleep. "Morning."

She turns to me, a small smile on her lips. "Morning."

I point to the bathroom. "First shower?" Her smile fades as she nods, hoisting herself out of bed.

I'm not ready to say goodbye either, but there's nothing we can do. Both of our families are expecting us. We head to the airport in silence, holding hands the entire time.

At the security gate, we say our goodbyes. She throws her arms around me, holding on tight. "I'll miss you."

"I'll miss you too," I say, my voice cracking with emotion.

We kiss one last time before she heads to her gate. As I watch her walk away, my stomach drops. I don't want to let go of the weekend with her, but I can't convince her we're endgame by keeping her close.

When I land in Missouri, my family is waiting for me at the airport. I hug them all, happy to see them, but my mind is still on Violet. I try to push the thoughts aside, to focus on my family.

On the ride to my parent's place, I grab my phone and text Violet, letting her know I made it to Missouri safely. *I miss you already.* I hit Send before I can say anything more serious.

My phone immediately buzzes: *Miss you, too. Have fun with your family.*

I smile, feeling a little better knowing she's thinking of me, too. *You too*, I shoot back.

I'll be in Texas at the weekend. Sure, this is our first separation as a couple. But we've known each other for a long time. I'm sure I'm making more of this than I need to.

Violet

A DRIVER PICKS ME up at the airport, holding a sign with my name. I grin. I already know what my parents are doing. My mother's home, making sure that the house is perfect for whatever Norman Rockwell–style Christmas dinner she has planned. My father is working, either at home or at his office.

Sure enough, when the driver drops me at my parents' house and I step inside, the foyer is like something out of Southern Living. My mother's taste is impeccable, and she prides herself on execution. Sometimes, I want to tell her I'd rather things weren't so perfect if it meant having more of her.

"Violet!" she exclaims, coming in from the study. "I knew I heard the car wheels on the drive." She folds me in her arms, and she smells exactly the same as I remember—like Chanel No. 5. The scent fills me with nostalgia, and I squeeze her back. She might frustrate me sometimes, but I do love her.

"Hello, Mama."

She pulls back to look at me, and her gaze misses nothing. "You look skinny. Are you eating enough? Getting enough sleep?"

I don't bother responding, because she can probably tell what the answers are. She knows I sleep for crap, and if I tell her I've been working too much and probably not eating right, she'll disapprove. So I stay silent.

She sighs and pats my cheek. "I'm so glad to have you home."

We link arms, and she leads me down the hall toward the den, pointing out all the decorations she's put up for the holiday season. I can't help but admire her attention to detail. Everything is perfect, down to the last pinecone. I wonder how long it took her to get everything just right. I nod and smile, letting her talk and lead me around her immaculate home.

My father is reading the paper at the table in the kitchen. Probably the Wall Street Journal. He still prefers the paper to the internet.

He looks up as we enter, and he grins. "Baby girl! So good to see you. How was your flight?" He sets the paper down, stands up, and hugs me. He smells like aftershave and the peppermints he has crunched ever since he quit smoking, and I feel like a little girl again.

"It was fine, Daddy. How are you?"

"Just trying to keep your mother from going overboard with all this Christmas stuff." He folds his arms, and my mother frowns at him.

"Stanley, you know I've been working with a party planner for New Year's Eve." She scowls at him. "She's done most of the work. I just supervise."

He winks at me. "I know, baby. I appreciate you." He's not lying.

My parents couldn't be more different. My father is a numbers man—he loves diving into the intricacies of the stock market, crunching numbers, and playing with investments. He's in his element when he's working long hours at the office, and it's clear he gets a thrill out of it.

My mother, on the other hand, has no interest in any of that. She's all about hosting parties, decorating, and creating warm spaces for family and friends to gather in. She loves making sure every detail is just right, from the flowers to the table settings to the lights strung around the windows.

The two of them make it work. They understand each other and respect one another's passions, even though they may seem completely different on the surface. Just like me and Hunter. I smile.

"Your mother tells me you have a new beau." Dad's brows furrow. "Tell me more."

"Hunter and I started dating." When I originally told Mom, it wasn't true. But I suppose now it is.

"Hunter Mason, correct?" He waits for me to confirm. "I met him at your graduation, didn't I?" I can see the wheels turning in my father's head.

"Yes." Irritation flares, but I tamp it down.

My parents met a lot of people at graduation, and at the time, Hunter and I weren't more than friends. Looking back on it, I realize I probably downplayed how close we actually were. Why did I do that? It's not because he's a guy. I have a lot of male friends. Ultimately, though, it isn't their fault if I didn't make him more memorable—it's mine.

"He'll be coming to the party this weekend?" he asks.

I nod. "Yes. He's with his family today, and then he'll be in Colorado. Then his game this weekend is home, and then he'll fly here." When I explain it like that, it sounds like forever until I'll see him again, even though it'll only be a week.

"I'm glad he'll be coming. I look forward to getting to know him better." My father smiles, and I know he's being honest.

"It's a shame he couldn't come for longer," my mother says with a breezy wave. "But I have a lot of gatherings to attend and entertaining to do. It'll keep us busy, and I'm certain he wouldn't be interested in that stuff."

I keep my face impassive. She doesn't overtly say it's because he wouldn't fit into those things, but that's how I hear it.

I point upstairs. "I'm going to go unpack, and I might lie down for a bit before lunch." When my mom's face falls, I soften the words with an apologetic shrug. "Early flight. I'm exhausted. But I'll be ready for Christmas festivities in an hour or so."

Then I fold her into a hug. She squeezes me back. After I hug my father, too, I head up the back stairs and down the hall to my bedroom.

I'm struck by how clean and organized my room is. The bed is made, the curtains are drawn, and it smells like lavender—my mom's signature home fragrance. I can't help but smile as I remember the countless times she would nag me about keeping my room tidy. It's funny how we never really appreciate those things until we're older.

I flop down on the bed and close my eyes, feeling the weight of exhaustion settle in. My mom was right—it's been a while since I've been home. But as much as I love my parents and miss them, I'm already looking forward to seeing Hunter again.

Christmas day is wonderful, but the second I wake up the day after, a flurry of social engagements begins. There's a breakfast with a local women's league. We attend a garden party at my mother's best friend's house. I'm grilled by my mother's closest friends about my career and my dating. It's obvious they're trying to figure out exactly how close to a wedding I am and if I plan to move back to Austin anytime soon. I do my best not to give away how little I want to be there.

I hoped I would see my friend Melanie. Her mom usually drags her to these things, too. But she's home with her daughter. I didn't know she had a baby. I'm sure I talked to her in the spring.

By the third day at home, I need some time. I tell my mother I have some work to do and hide in my father's office. I have work I can do, because I wanted to look at the program I've been writing.

An hour later, my father comes in. "Hiding?" He glances at his watch. "You only made it a couple of days. You're getting soft, baby."

If my mother and I have a complicated relationship, my relationship with my father is the exact opposite. When I was younger, he deferred to my mother's influence, probably because I was a girl. But with my love of finance and math, we have always spoken the same language.

I don't want to admit he's right, so I point to my computer. "I'm working on something."

He sits in the chair across from me. "For Kellerman?"

I shake my head. "My project with PLG ended last week. This is something of my own."

He raises his eyebrows. "Your own, huh? A program?"

We've talked before about my love of coding. My father has a brain for numbers, and he's a brilliant financial analyst, but programming has always frazzled him. "It is."

He points to the liquor cabinet. "Drink?"

I glance at my watch. "It's only four o'clock, Dad."

He holds a finger to his lips. "Yes, but it's five o'clock in New York, and you're probably still used to that time, anyway, so..."

I laugh at him. "Sure, sounds good."

I don't even have to ask what he's going to pour for me. My father drinks bourbon. He hands me a glass with a couple of fingers' worth and lifts his own to me. "To having my baby home."

"Cheers, Dad." I take a sip, and the burn is familiar. I've been sipping bourbon in my father's office since I was a teenager.

"So tell me about this program." He settles into the chair in front of me.

Others have asked me about my project, but most of them don't understand the specifics. They might get pieces of the financial aspects, or they might understand coding or programming, but my father is the head of a hedge fund. He's invested in startups, he's been involved in mergers, and he's well-versed in portfolio management.

I explain the basics of my program. The performance-reporting platforms on the market don't offer enough customization for smaller family offices. I tell him about how I'm structuring my platform, and we chat about the different options for its use.

When I'm done, he studies me as he finishes his bourbon. "What do you think your start-up costs are?"

I laugh, shaking my head. "Oh, I have no idea..."

"Why not?" My father isn't laughing. His brow furrows. "It's obvious you've thought about this. You haven't created a business plan?" He's serious.

"I'm working at Kellerman." We've talked about this step in my career for years. When I decided on my majors, my father gave me his input. Finance and computer science, so I could get an entry-level job like the one I have at Kellerman's. Now, he wants me to throw that away on a risk?

He waves his hand. "It's a consulting firm. You're between jobs, aren't you?"

"Well, yes... but they pay for my healthcare—" We talked about benefits.

He snorts. Actually snorts. "You're a brilliant mathematician and coder, Violet Jean. You're worrying about benefits?"

I scowl at him. "You know, regular people worry about that stuff. And you told me to worry about benefits."

"You're not regular people." He waves me off.

I sit up straight and blink at him. "Yes, I am."

He narrows his eyes at me. "Violet, how'd you do in high school?"

"You know how I did."

"Humor me. Recite it off, like you're in an interview."

"Valedictorian. Math Honor Society. French Honor Society. Cheerleading. Gymnastics. Homecoming Court. Robotics Club. National Honor Society. Chorus." I rattle off the things I remember. "Oh, I was on Debate Club for a hot second, too."

"And at Chesterboro, you graduated summa cum laude, with a dual major, in conjunction with Pennsylvania University, in finance and computer science. You were vice president of finance for Delta Alpha, a national sorority. And you helped with the robotics club at the local high school." He points at me. "Don't forget that."

"My classes kept me busy in college." I shrug. "Not as much time for clubs and stuff."

"My point is, you're not regular. You worked very hard, and you're an incredibly accomplished woman. And now you've built this program."

I've always known my father is proud of me, but this feels different. As he recites my achievements, it's matter of fact, as if he's reading from my resume. This doesn't sound like empty bragging—he means every word. The realization fills me with happiness.

He continues, unaware. "I can think of at least two different investors who would be interested in this, plus myself, of course."

"Are you serious?" Even as I ask, I can tell he is. My dad wouldn't joke about business. I laugh, closing the lid on my computer. "I can't just... start a company. I'm twenty-two years old."

"So what?" It's his turn to shrug.

"So..." I don't have a good argument. "I guess I assumed I could sell the program. Some day. But I figured I wasn't ready to do something like that yet. I just graduated from college. I've only got six months of actual work experience." Shaking my head, I set the computer on the stand next to me. "What do I know about running a company?"

"Nothing yet," he says. "But that doesn't mean you shouldn't go for it. Because you're a sharp woman. If you don't know something, you know how to find the information you need. I don't doubt you'll figure this out, too."

"Dad..."

"And you have me to help you." He puffs up. "I'm no slouch either. Just think about it. There's no rush."

"Well, PLG wants to sign me on for another contract. To build something like this for them."

He considers. "That would be a safer move. Much less risky to let them handle the upfront costs. But do you want to hand over your hard work to them?" When I don't immediately respond, he smiles knowingly. "Exactly."

"I just don't know." It's a huge gamble, but now that he's suggested it, my brain has latched on. He's right. If someone is going to make money from my hard work, why shouldn't it be me?

"Let's revisit this. But think about it, okay?" He stands, collects my glass, and heads for the door. "And don't stay in here too long. Your mother was so excited you were coming home to visit."

I nod. Because I know he's right. I'm avoiding her. I collect my things, carry them into my bedroom, and tuck them away before going in search of my mother again. But my conversation with my father stays with me.

Hunter

My mom outdoes herself with Christmas dinner, and we all eat too much and laugh a lot. I love being surrounded by my siblings. It's hard to believe we used to fight all the time. Two of my younger siblings are in college, but they're both home for the holidays. It's rare to get all of us together, especially with me on the East Coast. The rest of my siblings are still in middle school and high school, so they're all off. It's nice to be with everyone. I miss them being so far away.

As a farmer's wife, my mom isn't a stranger to preparing enormous meals, but she outdoes herself on the holidays. The day after Christmas, she puts out a full-scale feast and invites all of our local extended family to attend. My father's brothers come by with their families. Their farms are next to my parents, so we see them often. But something about a house full of relatives always feels festive. It's happy chaos, with kids running everywhere and people talking.

When my siblings and I help clear dishes, my mother catches me at the sink. She presses a holiday towel into my chest. "You get to dry," she tells me. It's not a request. In my experience, farmer's wives could have been field generals in past lives, and my mother is no exception.

I step up to the sink next to her. She hands me a casserole dish. "You and Violet are dating now," she says.

My mom doesn't mince words. But sometimes her conversation tactics feel a little like shock and awe. "Yes." It's true, I suppose, after this weekend.

"Violet dated Nate Graham, didn't she? Your junior year?"

My mother doesn't forget anything. She knows the answer to this. "She did."

"How's it going?" Of all of my friends from college, I've probably talked the most about Violet to my mother. Now that she and I are dating, I wonder if that wasn't a mistake.

"It's good, Mom." I set the dry dish behind me on the table. It's one of her Christmas set. I don't know if she's leaving it out or storing it.

She hands me a platter, holding on to it until I meet her gaze. "Don't give me all the details at once, Hunter." She rolls her eyes before sticking her hands back in the sudsy water.

I chuckle. "Violet's great. There's really nothing to say."

She hums noncommittally. "When do we get to meet her?" My parents couldn't come to Chesterboro for my graduation in May. Between the farm and my siblings, they couldn't get away.

"I don't know. She lives in Philadelphia, too. And her family lives in Austin."

"She's always welcome here, you know," she tells me, glancing up at me. At five-four, my mother is only average height. But me and my siblings seemed to get the height from my father's side. My two brothers and I are all over six feet, and my sisters are all above average for girls. But though Mom is the shortest now, she's still the one in charge around here.

"I'll make sure she knows."

"You can bring her after the season's over," she tells me.

"Mom, that might not be until the summer."

"It'll be busy, but we would love to see her."

"It's not that," I mumble. "It's just..."

"What?" she asks. I meet her gaze, and we pause. Because I don't know if we'll still be together in the summer. It's not me I worry about. I can't imagine not wanting to be with her. But Violet's gun-shy. I'm forcing myself to live in the moment.

"Nothing." I shake my head. "The summer. We'll try to visit then."

We go back to the dishes, working in companionable silence. Well, as silent as it can be when the house is full of family. After a few long moments, my mother says, "You're a sweet kid, Hunt."

"Thanks, Mom." I have no idea where this is going.

"I just mean... you're quiet, and sometimes people think that means reserved or cold. But it doesn't with you. Just be careful with your heart, okay?" She squeezes my arm, and I can feel her wet hand through my sleeve.

"All right, Mom," I tell her, because what else can I say to something like that?

After dinner, my family sits around my parents' gigantic fireplace with coffee and Baileys. As usual, I'm mostly a spectator to my family's hijinks. Later, I beat my brothers at some Nintendo game, and I catch my mom watching me. I wonder if she's worrying about me having my heart broken.

I wonder if I should worry, too.

We lose both of our games in Colorado the week after Christmas. That's three in a row, and Coach is pissed. I hate to blame the goalie, but Nate's been playing like shit. We could have a piece of Swiss cheese in the net, and it would catch more pucks. He's distracted and slow to respond, and it's getting worse. When he leaves the ice after the second game in Colorado, the fans there mock-cheer him. His mood is black in the locker room.

If we were still friends, I'd try to help him shake it off. But we don't talk now. Anything I say to him would appear patronizing, so I keep my mouth shut. I notice that no one else approaches him, either. Apparently, Nate's not making friends here.

When the locker room clears, Coach pulls me aside. "I just wanted to let you know, Mason… Huck is scheduled to return next week, after the holiday."

"He is, sir?" I'm surprised he's telling me this.

"His recovery has gone much better than anyone expected." He raps his knuckles on the clipboard in front of him. "His physical therapist has written her support. He needs to clear through the doctors here, but we're hopeful. It'll be good to have him back."

"It will." Huck and I aren't friends, but I like the guy. He brings good energy to the locker room.

"I also wanted to know if you've ever played center."

"Center, Coach?" I fold my arms, my stance wide. "Well, sure. But not since high school and club hockey. It's been a while." When I joined the Chesterboro team, there were already three solid centers, so the coach there asked me to play wing. I've always been a team player. I did what I needed to do.

"In high school, huh?" He considers. "I want you to play center for us in the next couple of games." He matches my stance, folding his arms. "We need you."

"Um, sure. Whatever you need." My brow furrows. "But what about…?"

"There's been a trade. We'll announce it in the morning. But we'll be down a center within the next twenty-four hours."

I'm always alarmed to hear management talk about trades or sending players down to the minors. It's just business to them, but even if it doesn't seem like they made a quick decision, some guy's life is about to change. We had all our centers here in Colorado tonight. That means someone is going to wake up tomorrow and need to pack up his life in Philadelphia.

I swallow. "Of course. I'll play wherever you need me to play, Coach."

He claps me on the shoulder. "Good man." He moves like he's going to leave.

"Coach?"

Pausing, he lifts his brow. "Yeah?"

"How does this affect my trade talks?" I don't want to overstep here, but things have changed for me. Something's started with Violet, and it's new. I don't know where it's going. I'm not an anxious guy, but it would be nice to remove some of the uncertainty from my situation.

"Only time will tell." He shakes his head apologetically. "There are a lot of moving pieces right now. Restructuring is always painful, and management is exploring a variety of options. I just know that I need you to play center on Saturday."

"Of course." Usually, I would leave it at that. I do as I'm told, and I know my place. It's my first year in the league, and I'm the lowest man on the ladder. Still, I need to say something. "I'm happy to stay in Philadelphia, though, if the team would have me. I like the city, and I like the team. So if Philadelphia remains an option, I'd be happy to stay as well." I pause. "I'm dating someone. She's special." I clamp my mouth shut. Even this much feels like too much to ask.

Coach Hargreeves studies me for so long that I'm afraid I've overstepped. Finally, he nods. "Thanks for letting me know, kid. I'll make sure we keep that in mind."

I nod. At least I said my piece. At my locker, I continue gathering my stuff, hurrying now so I'm not late.

"Mason." Duke, our captain, stands next to me, his bag slung over his shoulder. "Real quick. I just wanted to drop by and thank you for stepping up. I appreciate that you're willing to fill a void for us."

"No problem. Happy to help."

I think he's going to walk away, but he doesn't. Instead, he lowers his voice so that I'm the only one who can hear him. "Listen, I didn't mean to overhear your conversation with Coach, but..." He shrugs. "I just want you to know that I hope you stay here in Philadelphia, too." He glances around to make sure no one is paying any attention to us before he continues. "I don't plan to be here next year, but that doesn't mean I don't care about this organization. You remind me a lot of myself." He gives me a punch on the arm that would have hurt if I weren't still wearing my shoulder pads. "You're like this city. Hardworking, no-nonsense. And that's what I told the coaching staff when they asked me about it the other day. I told them I could see you wearing the C on your jersey someday. Just wanted to tell you that."

I glance up at him, cocking my head. It's hard not to admire Duke. In a lot of ways, we're similar. We're both grinders. Neither of us says much. But he demands respect in the locker room and out.

"Thank you, man. I appreciate that," I say. Because I don't know what else to say. He didn't need to say any of that. Duke's a man of few words. So why the heart-to-heart now?

He nods and leaves without another word.

I have little time to consider these conversations because I need to make the bus to the airport. It's not until we're standing on the tarmac, preparing to board the plane home, that I can pull my phone out of the side pocket. We're at home on Saturday, and then I'll fly into Austin after my game. New Year's Eve is Sunday, and I'll need to fly back to Philadelphia on Monday morning to play that night. It'll be a quick trip and a lot of travel, but I promised Violet I'd make it to the party, and I don't plan to let her down.

It's after eleven in Austin, and Violet might not be awake. But I drop her a text to let her know I'm thinking of her: *I miss you. Hope you're having fun with your parents.*

Her typing dots appear and then a message: *I can't wait to see you.*

Everything okay? I ask.

My mom is a lot. She sends an emoji of a goofy face, and I smile.

So you come by it honestly, huh? I tease.

Watch your mouth, Mason. I could take you, she replies with an angry face.

A grin splits my face. *I'm sorry. I'll be there soon.*

I repeat—I can't wait.

Closing my texting app, I follow my teammates onto the plane. Only a few more days.

Violet

Hunter doesn't get into Austin until late Saturday night. He looks exhausted, so I get him settled in his room. But I don't want to go to sleep right away. We curl up together, and I ask him a million questions about his week. This wasn't the first time we'd been apart for a week, but it was the first time since we slept together. It felt different somehow.

My parents are at the yacht club for dinner with friends, so they don't meet him officially until the next morning. Or rather, meet him officially as my boyfriend. My dad and Hunter hit it off. Neither of them is a man of many words, but they appreciate each other's straightforward personalities.

My mother is another story. "So this is your first year playing for the Tyrants, correct?" She sips her coffee and stares at him over the rim. I didn't get to sleep until very late. So while I'm in an oversized sweatshirt, sleep shorts, and a messy bun, my mother is perfectly coiffed and ready for her day.

It doesn't appear to intimidate Hunter, though. He nods and finishes chewing a bite of his omelet before he answers. "Yes. I graduated from Chesterboro with Violet last year."

I scowl at my mother. She knows that. I can feel the undercurrent of their conversation across the table.

"What do you plan to do after your hockey career is over?"

I blow out an exasperated breath, rolling my eyes. "Mother. That's years from now."

She sets down her coffee mug, the picture of innocence. "I only mean that it's always good to have a plan. Professional sports isn't a lifetime profession."

I can only glare at her. She's never once asked me about my long-term plans, but here she is interrogating my boyfriend about his. It's the worst kind of hypocrisy. Especially because she never asked Nate, in the entire year we dated, what his plans were for after hockey.

Hunter wipes his mouth. "I'm not exactly sure what happens after hockey," he says, pretending there's no tension at the table at all. "I have a degree in agricultural science. My family owns a farm in Missouri. I hope I'll play hockey for a long time, but when it's over, I'll probably go home and work with them."

My mother barely represses her distaste. "What exactly does your family farm?"

Hunter doesn't seem to notice. "Soy and corn, mostly. My father has some cattle as well, and my uncle grows cotton." He shrugs.

"Soy and corn. Some cattle." My mother's eyes are wide. "Well, that sounds lovely." When she says "lovely," it sounds like she means horrifying.

My mouth drops open. I don't know what I plan to say, but my father jumps in and steers the conversation to more boring topics. As my dad gets her rundown of what needs to happen for the party, I try to control my irritation. I've been at home with my mother for the past week, and I've had to bite my tongue more often than I please. My flight leaves tomorrow morning, and I hate how much I'm counting down those minutes.

After lunch, I'm glad for all of my mother's last-minute preparations because they keep me distracted. My father begs off, retreating to his office with the excuse that something came up at work. I don't believe it, and I doubt my mother does either, but she lets him go, probably because she still has Hunter around, willing to do the literal heavy lifting. She sends me to manage the final decorations, and she puts Hunter in charge of helping the caterers.

When I escape to the kitchen around six o'clock, I find him shoveling appetizers into his face at the sink. His eyes are wide, and he pauses, a crepe halfway to his mouth. "Don't tell your mother."

I crack up. Then I glance behind me before stepping up next to him. "Only if I can have some."

He holds a crepe up to my lips. His brows lift in challenge. There are people scurrying around, so maybe he doesn't think I'll take it from him. But he's always been the one who shied from affectionate displays, not me.

Keeping eye contact with him, I take the mini-crepe into my mouth, letting my lips slide over his fingers. Heat lights in his gaze. I snag the appetizer plate from him and put it on the counter next to us. Then I lean into him, placing my arms around his waist. He gathers me against him and drops his mouth to mine.

I sigh, reveling in the contact as we kiss, pressed against each other, in my parents' kitchen. In the past, I've wanted Hunter around. When he's been out of town, I've looked forward to him coming home. But this week has been different. Not having him near felt like a physical ache, like a part of me was missing.

"Violet Jean." My mother's voice cuts in, and we break apart. Hunter keeps me tucked against his side, though.

"Yes, Mom." I face her, doing my best to keep my face serene.

"Why don't you and Hunter go get dressed if you're finished here?" She lifts her eyebrows, shakes her head, and strides off toward the dining room.

Hunter whistles under his breath. "Caught making out by your mother? I feel like I just got yelled at in school." He chuckles in my ear as he presses a kiss to my temple. "She's a real force of nature, isn't she?"

I snort. "You have no idea. But she's letting us off the hook for party preparations. Let's go before she changes her mind." I grab his hand, and we escape up the back stairs.

The party is going to begin at eight o'clock, so I have plenty of time to prepare. It's black tie, and I insisted I could wear something I already own, but my mom wasn't into it. We went shopping earlier in the week. It might have been the most fun I had with her. We had brunch, and she didn't appear disapproving once. After that, we strolled through the boutiques downtown. I settled on a long green chiffon gown with sheer sleeves. Tonight, I pin my hair up into a simple bun. Makeup is a smoky eye with a neutral lip because I plan to kiss Hunter at every opportunity, and dark lipstick is like glitter—it gets everywhere.

My mother insisted Hunter have his own room, and she put him in the guest room on the other side of the house. Because of course, she did. So I don't see him until I come downstairs before eight. He's waiting for me in the foyer, and he stands when he sees me. The appreciation on his face fills my stomach with warmth.

"You look amazing, pretty girl," he tells me, taking my hand and placing a kiss on it.

I wrap my arms around him and pull him close for a kiss. "And you are the most handsome man I've ever met."

It's the truth too. His tuxedo is classic, and nothing about what he's wearing stands out. But he makes it look better than any other man. Or maybe I just think he's that much better than everyone else.

Around us, the house is perfect. Everything is in place. My mom's done an impeccable job. I can't fathom the planning that goes into an event this size. There will be at least a hundred people here. But there's no way to miss the amount of work she's done and attention to detail in the surrounding preparations.

A string quartet warms up in the foyer, and I know Mom has a DJ in the great room for dancing later. In the sitting room next to the foyer, there's a full bar. The wait staff are poised in the kitchen, ready to distribute hor d'oeuvres.

My father and mother come downstairs, and I hug them both. "Mom, this is magnificent. You've done a beautiful job, as always." She looks lovely in a long silver gown, her blond hair arranged in a simple updo.

My mom kisses both of my cheeks. Her expression barely changes, but I know her. She's pleased. "Thank you, dear."

Our guests arrive shortly after eight, and it's a whirlwind. I introduce Hunter to my high school friends, and they all greet him happily. There's lots of hockey talk. There have been whispers that Austin might host its own expansion team. I don't think I realized how much excitement there was in my home city for the sport. My father never followed it. His sport of choice is football, and he watches the Longhorns religiously.

An hour into the party, my father cups my elbow as Hunter and I listen in on an intense conversation between a local representative and the president of a local bank. "Could I steal you away for a few minutes? I have some people I'd like you to meet."

Hunter nods, waving me away. "Of course," I say. I make my excuses, and then I follow him into his office.

Outside the door, he pauses. "I want you to keep an open mind, okay?"

When he opens the door, there are already four men inside. I glance at my father, and he smiles encouragingly, leading me forward. I recognized two of the men, but not the others.

My father closes the door behind us. "Violet, I'd like you to meet some of my business associates." He points to the first man on the left, an older gentleman with glasses. "You know Charles Steinberg. He's a stockholder of my hedge fund. And Marcus Middleton."

I nod to the attorney. I've met him a few times at my parents' country club. He works with my father on some of their ventures.

I shake hands with Charles and Marcus. "Happy New Year, gentlemen."

My father motions to the third man. "Violet, this is John Harlon. His family operates the Harlon Furniture chain."

I step forward to shake his hand as well. Harlon is a massive retail conglomerate with a presence in most large cities. "It's nice to meet you."

He smiles, his expression warm. "It's wonderful to meet you, Miss Tannehill. Your father has told us a lot about you and this wonderful new program you're developing."

I glance at my father. "Has he?"

Mr. Harlon nods as the last man steps forward. "I'm John's son, Jacob. I manage our family investment office."

A family investment office is an investment fund that manages the financial assets of a family or group of ultra-high-net-worth people. They hire experts to handle their wealth, customize their investments, and cater to their financial needs. It makes sense that a family like the Harlons would have one.

"It's wonderful to meet you too."

Jacob folds his hands in front of him. "Our family office has been looking for an alternative to our current reporting software. A lot of the investment management tools get us only so far. It sounds like the product you're developing is something we could use."

"Really?" My mind spins. All I keep going back to is how strange it is to be discussing financial software on New Year's Eve. But I guess hustlers have to hustle.

Marcus steps forward. "When your father talked about it on the golf course the other day, it sparked my interest as well. In the past, I've worked with two bright software developers to create reports for our company. Both of them have worked with large banks and corporations, but they've recently been looking for capital to strike out on their own. Your father and I wondered if you might be interested in discussing a joint venture. I don't know if it'll work for all of your individual goals, but it could be an interesting conversation."

I lift my hand. "I'm so sorry, gentlemen. This is sudden. I'm having a hard time keeping up."

My father gestures to the table at the wall. "I took the liberty of having some champagne sent in. Would you like some?" He motions for us to sit and turns to me. "Marcus, Jacob, and I were golfing this week—"

I narrow my eyes. "On Thursday? You told Mom you had a meeting."

"I did," he says with a smile. "I met with Marcus and Jacob. On the course." I roll my eyes and chuckle. "I mentioned the software you were developing."

"You did?" It's no secret that business is conducted on golf courses, but I never thought my business would be discussed.

"Your father is very proud of you," Marcus interjects, offering a fatherly smile.

"And Jacob was particularly excited about what you said about customization," my father says. "To your performance platform."

"It's the drawback of most products we've seen," Jacob adds. "The programs aren't as flexible as we would prefer."

"And then Marcus and I were talking, and I remembered Charles was interested in pursuing venture capital opportunities."

"I have a few investors in mind as well." Charles smiles.

"So I wanted to get us all in the same room, to introduce you and see what you thought." My father sits beside me and takes a sip of his drink.

"And you figured that all out while you were playing a round of golf?" They shrug or nod at me as if such decisions are commonplace there. My gaze circles the room. "Well, I guess you all would be interested in seeing my program?" I've tinkered with programming my whole life. Teachers and professors have praised my work, but this is something different. These men have the influence and resources to help me take my creations to the next step. The prospect sends a thrill coursing through me.

My father cocks his head. "I think everyone here is interested in hearing what you could offer."

I motion toward the door. "Then let me run upstairs and grab my laptop."

Hunter

I'm with one of Violet's friends, explaining how an expansion team could benefit the Austin area when Violet returns. It's been almost half an hour since her father dragged her away. I was just beginning to worry if everything was okay. She doesn't say anything when she rejoins us, only steps next to me and loops her arm with mine. I squeeze her fingers, but when I glance down at her face, something is obviously wrong. Her eyes have that faraway look in them. It's the look that says she's thinking about a million things.

At the next stop in the conversation, I place my hand on the small of her back. "If you'll excuse us for a moment," I say to her friends. Violet allows me to guide her to an alcove in front of the library. The entire downstairs is full of people, but most of the party is going on in the entertaining spaces and outside, so there are only a couple of people here. I rub my arms over her shoulders. "Spill it. What's up?"

"What?"

I offer her side-eye. "You've got overthinking face on. Out with it. What's on your mind?"

Sighing, she covers my hands, squeezing my fingers. "My father introduced me to a few men who want to invest in my performance-reporting software." There's no emotion in her explanation.

She could be telling me that her father introduced her to the person who cleans his car.

"Investors? That's wonderful." I fold her in a hug, kissing the top of her head. "That sounds like an amazing opportunity." When we talked about her program, I could tell she didn't like the idea of sharing it with PLG or Kellermans. I can't say I blame her. She works too hard and is too smart to let other people steal her thunder.

I step back, but when I meet her gaze, it's troubled. She bites her lip. "It is. Or would be. I'm not exactly sure if I want to do it."

"What? Why not? You told me before Christmas that you weren't happy with how PLG wanted you to use your technology."

"That's true," she concedes, wrapping her arms around her waist. "But this… It's so much more than I expected. And so fast…" She shakes her head, glancing over my shoulder.

I might not know exactly what she's thinking right now, but I know that if I try to guess, I'll be wrong. Instead of putting myself through that, I open the door to the library. It's empty, so I snag her hand and pull her inside. This is one of my favorite rooms in the house. They covered the walls, from floor to ceiling, with books. There are a few comfortable chairs stationed around the space, with plenty of reading lights and places to put a drink or snack. I could spend days in this room.

I lead her to a chair and have a seat, then pull her into my lap. She comes willingly, curling up in her beautiful green gown and dropping her head onto my shoulder. I smooth a strand of loose hair off her face. "Why don't you walk me through all the things that are going through your mind right now?"

It's a long moment before she says anything, but I don't rush her. Hell, with all the stuff that occupies her thoughts, it probably takes time to sort through it. Finally, she sighs. "I set up a conversation with two other software developers my father's friend knows. They're working on developing financial software too. But I don't know them, and I don't know what their plans were. They might not fit with what I wanted to do."

"Or they might. If they don't, you don't have to work with them, right?" I can't imagine, though. I'm an acquired taste, but everyone loves Violet.

"I guess not. But what if I'm wrong?" She leans forward to meet my eyes, and I hate how unsure she looks. "I think that's what's bothering me. There are so many options. When I started working on this, it was just fun. Something I was doing to keep my brain busy when I couldn't sleep. Now some people want to give me money—like, a lot of money—to develop it. People want to meet me to talk about design."

"There are a lot more people involved in it." I'm trying to follow along, to understand what's wrong.

"Yes. But I don't think it's the people. It's the... expectations." She worries her bottom lip with her teeth. "What if it doesn't work?"

"Then it doesn't. Then you find something else." Her eyes widen, and I shrug. "We're twenty-two, Violet. We're in store for lots of ups and downs yet, aren't we?"

She scowls. "But I'll have given up my job at Kellerman, just to fail. And what if it fails and I've lost my father's friends their capital investment?"

"That's kind of the point of venture capital, isn't it?" I remind her gently. "It's not a guaranteed investment."

"But those are important business relationships for him. He's known some of them for years, and what if I cause a rift between them somehow?" She's getting riled up, worrying about the pitfalls.

"He wouldn't have introduced you to them and talked about this with them if he didn't believe in it—in you," I tell her quietly.

She sighs again. "I know." She tucks her head back on my shoulder. There's a pause. Then she says, "I'm going to screw this up."

I burst out laughing, and she glares up at me. "I'm sorry," I tell her. "It's just that when faced with a bunch of exciting prospects, you've managed to tangle yourself up until you're convinced you're going to screw up." I squeeze her. "Maybe you'll mess it up, but what if you don't? What if you kill it?"

She shifts, still on my lap, but now she searches my face. "They might want me to move here. Back to Texas." The words drop into the space between us, and my laughter fades. "The developers they are introducing me to are in here, in Austin." She waits a beat. "And you're in Philadelphia."

I open my mouth to tell her about my trade possibilities. But the words don't come out. I'm not supposed to talk about it. That's what Coach said. Confidential means secret.

It isn't only that, though. Whether or not I'm traded, I don't want her to make decisions like this—huge decisions—because of me. I don't have a clue where I could go or even if I would go. These need to be her choices. When we agreed to our fake relationship, I knew our time could be limited. But I didn't expect it to be cut short because of her career. I expected it to be mine. It doesn't matter, though, as I tell her the truth. "No matter where we are—Philadelphia, Austin, Seattle, hell, anywhere—it won't change how I feel about you."

I want to tell her I love her, that I've been in love with her for a long time. But I'm still not sure it's the right time. I don't want her to read anything unintended into it when I tell her those words. I certainly don't want her to think I'm trying to sway her in any direction, even while every possessive instinct I have screams to influence her, to never leave her side. "We can make this work, no matter where we are. I promise."

She cups my face in her hands and pulls my mouth to hers. The kiss she gives me is wild. I want to tell her that everything is going to be okay, but her eyes say she's not so certain. I'm not sure what to say to convince her, so I pour everything into our kiss.

When she pulls away, I hold her close. After a long minute, she moves to stand, and I follow her. "We should get back," she says.

I nod and allow her to pull me toward the door. But just before we leave, she stops. I barely have a moment to brace myself as she launches into my arms.

I gather her close, and she kisses me again. This time, it's confident, and it matches the smile she gives me at the end. "You should dance with me, Bossy. I got all fancied up."

"Let's go, pretty girl."

It's nearly three in the morning when the Tannehills say goodbye to the last of their guests. Violet's mother is still wide awake, cleaning up and taking stock of things. I wonder if Violet inherited her ability to run on next-to-no sleep from her mother.

Earlier, I hoped I could creep up to Violet's room to spend some time with her before I leave tomorrow. But when she kisses me sleepily and heads up the backstairs, I wander to my room on the other side of the house.

Exhaustion hits me as soon as I see the bed. I strip off my tux, draping it over a chair in the corner, and climb into the sheets in my boxers. Thanks to this past week's crazy travel schedule, I pass out as soon as my head hits the pillow.

The first strains of sun stream through the window when my door creaks, waking me. I'm groggy as Violet slips inside, wearing a pair of short pajama shorts and a T-shirt whose collar has been cut off to make the opening oversized, leaving one shoulder exposed.

She doesn't say anything, only slides under the covers next to me. I'm already reaching for her, and I curve her body into mine, fitting our limbs together. When we're snuggled up, we both sigh.

"I missed you," she whispers, pressing her cheek into my chest.

"Same." I press my lips to her hair, inhaling the smell of her shampoo.

When her fingers press into the muscles of my lower back, I groan. I'll never get enough of her touch, her taste, her smell. I reach for the hem of her shirt, tugging it over her head. She isn't wearing a bra, so I cup her breast in my hand, running my thumb over it. She gasps, and her mouth finds mine.

What follows is a flurry of movement as we drag clothes off or aside. It's only been a week, but it feels like so long since we've been together like this. When we're naked and our bare skin touches, we sigh. But it isn't enough for either of us.

"Vi, I need to be inside you."

"Yes," she breathes. I have enough sense to snag a condom out of my overnight bag, but my hands shake when I put it on. In the early morning light, Violet catches my eye. With sure fingers, she takes over for me.

With our eyes still holding, we come together in one movement. I hold her against me as I try to keep our pace steady, but it's not long before we're out of control, surging against each other. Our movements are frantic. When she cries out, squeezing around me, my release tackles me. What follows is blissful emptiness.

I gather her against me as our breathing evens out. She seems to doze off, but maybe we just both want to enjoy the quiet together without saying anything.

I fly to Philadelphia in a few hours. We have a game this afternoon and one tomorrow. Violet plans to stay in Austin, to speak with the developers her father wants her to meet. If things work out with them, if she starts a company here and leaves Kellerman's, this will be our reality. Long distance.

When trades came up last month, I assumed we would be here, too. Except I would be the one away from her in Philadelphia. Back then, I figured if we ended up in a long-distance relationship, that would be a success. But now, it feels like less of a triumph.

We haven't put any labels on what's happening between us. I'm the only one who's gone anywhere close to stating my intentions—last night when I told her we could make things work, no matter what. She didn't respond, though, except for a hot kiss.

Maybe I'm borrowing trouble. She hasn't made any decisions about Kellerman or her program yet. There will be time to talk about these details.

I pull her tighter against my side, tucking her head on my chest. Last night, I meant what I said. I plan to do whatever it takes to make things work with her.

Violet

Tuesday morning, I call Caitlyn and make an excuse to stay in Austin another day. My meeting with the two developers Marcus knows goes better than I imagined. I wasn't sure what to expect. My pessimistic side had me convinced this was a dead end.

But I'm charmed by the developer, Amanda. She's creative and progressive. She has very little financial knowledge, but she doesn't pretend she knows much about it. When we talk, she defers to her partner, Tareek, for specialist knowledge. But her coding is elegant, and she takes directions well. Tareek is serious. But he holds the accounting knowledge I don't have. I'm well-versed in finance, but he fills the voids in my expertise.

By the end of the conversations, I believe the three of us could create something interesting. I just need a few more days to work through the details. Tareek and Amanda are in Austin. Amanda's newly married, and Tareek's family is local. If I decide to work with them, I'll need to brooch telecommuting or I'll never be able to see Hunter.

I fly back to Philadelphia, and I'm there by early afternoon. I have my car take me directly to Kellerman, wheeling my luggage into the office behind me.

It doesn't surprise me when Caitlyn calls me in. "Close the door behind you," she tells me.

I sink into the seat in front of her desk. I've been up since six. Add in the time change, and I'm dragging.

"I hope you had a good vacation." My boss starts our conversation with pleasantries.

"It was lovely, thank you."

"Wonderful. Mine too," she says even though I didn't ask. "The paperwork came from PLG, and their terms are similar to your last agreement. It's the same NDA." She pushes a stack of papers to me. "It's all here. With the pay increase."

I sit up and drag the contract toward me with trepidation. Allowing my hands to rest on it, I take a deep breath. "Would you mind if I took these home with me? I just wanted to read through the details."

Caitlyn's eyebrows drop. "Well, I was hoping you could sign them today. The company wanted to get this sorted out as soon as possible."

"I see." I tap my fingers along the stack.

"Is there a problem?" she asks.

I shake my head. "No. I just... I didn't expect it to come so soon. It's been a long day of traveling, and I didn't sleep well last night. I only wanted a clear head to read before signing."

Caitlyn raps her knuckles on the desk, considering my request. "Fine. But I need them by the end of the week. We have a tight deadline to meet." She waves her hand. "Why don't you head home and get some rest? Tomorrow, we can go over questions."

I thank her and gather up the paperwork before exiting her office. When I get to my desk, I place the small packet on top of my empty workspace. Next to me, my luggage is propped against the cubicle wall. Around me, the buzz of the office continues, completely unconcerned that I'm not doing anything.

I worked my butt off in college—double major, honors, all the accouterments. This job at Kellerman Consulting was supposed to be my jumping-off point. It's one of the top five consulting firms in the country. Entry-level jobs are competitive.

I've only been here six months. This was my endgame. Kellerman was everything I wanted. It was finance and programming, my chance to do something I always wanted to do. I would work at Kellerman for a few years. I would create some connections, and perhaps find my way into a bigger company. In all my scenarios, I spent years learning the ropes at consulting and financial institutions until I was ready. I don't know how I was supposed to know I was ready. And I never asked what I was getting ready for.

Now I'm considering throwing it all away. It feels irresponsible, but I can't see a way forward here. It feels like I'm working toward someone else's goals.

I need to take this leap to work with Amanda and Tareek. It's a chance to build something from scratch, to be in control. I don't want someone else to take credit for my ideas, and that's what would happen if I worked with PLG again.

What does that mean for my relationship with Hunter? If my partners work in Austin, I will need to be there at least sometimes. But not all the time, I'm sure. There are so many options for telecommuting now, and our line of work doesn't require us to be sitting in a room, talking. We do everything on the computer. I'll just need to hammer out the details with them. There's no reason I can't stay in Philadelphia and telecommute. Only fly to Austin when it's necessary. It might be difficult, but I'll manage it.

Hunter's worth it.

I take the contract home with me and spend the rest of the afternoon poring over the details. The more I read it, the more I realize that taking that job—staying with the status quo—is the wrong decision for me. Even before the workday is over, I email Caitlyn and call out of work tomorrow. I need a day to figure out my telecommuting with Amanda and Tareek, create a real business plan, and firm up funding details with our investors.

Our investors. The words give me chills.

Decided, I shower off the traveling funk. The Tyrants have a home game, and then I'm supposed to meet Hunter at the Pearl. I can't wait to tell him everything.

I feel light as I walk the few blocks to the Pearl. Inside, I spy Olivia and Lyle on the balcony, so I head up there. It isn't until I reach the top of the staircase that I see that Nate's with them.

My good mood dims, but I take the chair next to Lyle. Unwrapping my scarf from my neck, I greet everyone and then point at the television on the wall. It's playing the Tyrants game highlights. They won.

"Nate, didn't you play tonight?" I ask.

Lyle groans. "I'm going home. I've already heard this." He pushes his chair back, and I resist the urge to ask him to stay. The last thing I want to do is spend any time alone with Olivia and Nate. But he's gone before I can come up with a believable argument.

Nate downs whatever is in his glass. It looks like straight whiskey. "I fly out in the morning. Traded. To San Diego."

"You got traded?" He's only been in Philadelphia for a month.

"Huck Sokolov is back. They don't need me." He pushes his glass away from him, his mood dark. "I heard last week that they were excited about his recovery. I could see the writing on the wall." His mouth twists. "Been playing like shit because of it."

It's just like Nate to place the blame for his problems somewhere besides himself, but I don't say that.

Beside him, Olivia loops her arms with his. "It's going to be great. San Diego is beautiful. You'll see." Her voice is falsely upbeat, and her eyes are bright. "I love it there. I can't wait to visit you."

Nate grunts and Olivia appears stricken. My stomach turns for her. I remember that feeling. I don't think I recognized it when it was happening to me, but I can see it now.

Nate is too wrapped up in his own head to care about her. He motions to the server, requesting another drink. The girl hurries off.

"'Restructuring' they said. More trades coming this week, apparently." He glances at me, and the look on his face is mean. Instinctively, I brace myself. "Possibly Mason and Colt. Draft spots."

"Mason, like, Hunter?" I ask, the blood pounding in my ears.

He nods, holding my gaze. "He's been part of trade rumors this whole month. You didn't know about it?" He appears to be enjoying this.

I shake my head. The other people in the bar become a whirl of color and sound around me, but all I can hear are the words "trade rumors" on repeat in my mind.

"Well, I guess we're all surprised, then." He pushes back from the table. "I need to get back and pack."

Olivia reaches for him. "I'll come with you."

He shakes his head. "I'm not good company. Stay and have fun with your friend." It's a bullshit response. There's nothing in our relationship that says friendship and all of us know it.

Olivia doesn't appear deterred. "Well, I can drive you to the airport tomorrow," she says. "I'll ask Caitlyn for a few hours off."

It's obvious Nate wants to argue, but he doesn't. "Sure." They stand and embrace, but he's distant. Then he's gone.

The server arrives with his drink as we watch him head to the door downstairs. She tries to hide her irritation and fails.

"I'll take that," I tell her. No reason she should be out of a tab because Nate's a dick. She places it in front of me. "What is it?"

"Old-fashioned."

"Perfect." Nate and I always had similar tastes in alcohol. I swallow a sip. *Trade rumors, trade rumors...*

My eyes snag on Olivia, who is turning her martini around in her hands. Her gaze is far off, and she looks miserable. We're not friends, but just over a year ago, I remember feeling like her. Sure, it's different. Nate and I dated for a year, and Olivia has only started seeing him. But now that I look back on our relationship, I can see that Nate's no different from how he was with me. Still self-absorbed, immature.

Though I'll probably regret it, I offer Olivia a toast. "Can I give you some advice?"

She looks startled, like she forgot I was there. She considers me. "Sure."

"You don't deserve whatever you're telling yourself right now."

"What do you mean?"

"I mean, if you're thinking you did something that made him not want to see you in San Diego, you didn't. And he wasn't excited about you offering him a ride, but it has nothing to do with you. He doesn't recognize how inconvenient it is to take off work. He doesn't care that you want to do that so you can spend a couple more hours with him." I shake my head. "It's not you. It's him."

She blows out a breath and swallows her drink. "I don't know what you're talking about," she says with a breezy laugh.

Maybe she doesn't want to hear this right now. Or maybe she just doesn't want to hear it from me. Either way, I needed to say it. It's the truth. I spent a lot of months thinking Nate's choices were my fault somehow and blaming myself for how things ended. That was a waste of my time. He never took care of me or cared how I would feel when he left. Nate only cares about himself.

I lift my hands and drain my drink. "Okay." Setting the glass on the table, I stand. "I'm going to head home, too. I'm not really in the mood to be out."

She nods and offers me a distracted wave. Standing, I gather my things. I have my own bullshit to sort out. Like how my best friend, the man I've been sleeping with, didn't tell me he was the center of trade talks.

I don't read hockey forums. Hockey is fun to watch, but I've never been a puck bunny. It's only a coincidence that I spend so much time with hockey players and their significant others. If there's been any conversation on the forums, I missed it.

But Hunter would know about it. Our conversation on New Year's Eve comes back to me—his promise that we could make it work wherever we went.

He knew.

Hunter

For New Year's game on Monday, I play center and score twice. Still, it's a loss. Our defense breaks down, and Nate's performance was poor. The Philadelphia fans boo him as he skates off the ice. It's painful to watch.

But Tuesday night, Huck Sokolov is back. They call up our rookie goalie to back him up, leaving Nate off the roster. Duke shrugs and suggests they're giving Nate the night off.

Nothing changes for me. I play center again, and I'm more comfortable in the position. I've never been afraid of physical play, and I'm defense-minded. It's always been a good fit.

We win, thanks to Huck's impressive performance in goal. He's a wall, stopping every shot that comes his way. I score once, but it's the other line that shines tonight. They score three goals, and our defense holds strong, though there's still work they need to do. Overall, it's a total team effort, and we all celebrate in the locker room afterward. Everyone likes breaking a losing streak.

Colt and Rocco convince some guys to head to the Pearl afterward, and I don't need to be talked into it. I already planned on it. Violet's going to be there.

But when we reach the corner a block from the bar, Nate pushes through the Pearl's exit. His posture is rounded, like it's heavy, carrying the chip on his shoulder. He shuffles down the sidewalk toward us, and I brace myself. Something is wrong.

I don't like his smile as he heads toward us. He sticks out his hand. "Best of luck to you guys."

Rocco is the only one who reaches for him. "What are you talking about?"

"Traded," Nate offers. "To San Diego."

Rocco nods and shakes his hand, but he says nothing. Colt steps forward and repeats the gesture. "Good luck, man." Neither of them says anything else, heading inside the Pearl.

It's not a surprise. Nate didn't make friends in the locker room. But they leave me in the middle of the sidewalk with my former friend and the ex-boyfriend of the woman I love. I attempt civility.

Holding out my hand, I say, "Wish you the best in San Diego." A small part of me feels bad for him. It would suck to move twice in as many months. But any sympathy I mustered up dies when Nate leaves my hand between us. He crosses his arms over his chest.

"You didn't tell her you were getting traded?" He shakes his head, laughing. "I thought you were smarter than me, but I guess I was wrong."

I know immediately he's talking about Violet. My stomach hits the ground. "Nothing has happened yet."

"Right." He steps around me, opening his arms. "As big of a dumbass as I am."

He heads off the way I came, leaving me watching after him. When I turn back to the bar, Violet stands in the doorway, pulling her coat closed.

Of all of the ways Violet could have found out about my trade rumors, this is the worst one. I walk toward her slowly. "Violet, listen..."

She shakes her head. "I watched your game. You did great." Her smile is wooden. "You're getting the hang of playing center."

If she's pretending nothing's wrong, she's really upset. I lift my hands. "I haven't been traded yet."

She nods. "Yet." Her expression sickens me. She isn't angry. She doesn't even appear disappointed or betrayed. She just seems... resigned. "Nate said you've been the center of trade rumors for weeks."

Fucking Nate... "Coach told me around Thanksgiving, when Huck got hurt, that they might want to move me. It's no secret they're restructuring. Management seems to believe I could be worth money." She nods but doesn't say anything, so I continue. "But like I said, there's nothing concrete, and Coach insisted all trade conversations are confidential."

"Did you think I would tell anyone?" She tilts her head, narrowing her eyes. "Hell, it sounds like the people in the sports forums know more than I do."

Damn. This looks worse than it is. If I'd only told her sooner. "Violet—"

She shakes her head. "Listen, it's fine. Trades happen in hockey, right? Everyday stuff. I get it. And I get it, not being able to talk about it. I've signed NDAs." She hikes her tote on her shoulder. "I'm going to head home. It's been a long day, traveling and whatever." She points toward her apartment, stepping away from me.

I reach for her. "Wait, Vi. Let's talk about this. Just give me a second to explain—"

"That seems pointless. There's nothing really to explain, right? You haven't been traded. It's all just rumors right now." She lifts her eyebrows, her gaze challenging, as if daring me to tell her she's read this wrong. "Everything's all explained."

I open my mouth and close it. Because she's right, but wrong, too. I want to try to explain why I didn't say anything, but I can't find the words right now. I want to tell her I love her, that I can't even remember when I started to love her, and I can't imagine I would ever stop. I want to tell her it's all still rumors, and I haven't been traded. That I'm still here, right in front of her. But this isn't the right time for that, not when she's angry and hurt. Not when it seems like I lied to her.

"Let me walk you home," I finally say, stepping toward her.

She retreats, shaking her head. "That's okay. You just got here. Stay and have fun."

"I would rather be with you," I tell her honestly.

"And I'd rather be alone right now, Hunt." Her jaw firms, and there's steel in her eyes. "I need some space. I'll talk to you tomorrow." Without giving me a chance to say more, she spins on her heels and takes off toward her apartment.

I start to follow her, but I stop. What can I say? This isn't how I wanted her to find out about this. Hell, I've flirted with telling her about the trade rumors for weeks, and I didn't because I worried it would affect how our relationship was progressing. I thought maybe she wouldn't be as willing to give us a shot if she knew I was going somewhere. It was selfish of me, but I wanted this opportunity to find out if we could have something real together.

But in not telling her, was it real? I left out vital information. I didn't lie, but I didn't tell her the truth either.

Digging my hands into my hair, I pull and welcome the sting on my scalp. She asked for space, and I can give her that. Tomorrow, I'll tell her I'm sorry. I'll try to explain my thinking. I'll do whatever I can to fix this.

I don't feel like going into the Pearl now, so I head off toward my place. But it feels wrong to be walking away from her. And in the morning, everything changes.

Violet

I HURRY HOME. IT'S freezing cold, but I don't feel it at all. Maybe it's because I'm walking so fast, or it could be the anger coursing through me. Either way, I'm warm.

Amazingly, I get my apartment key to work on the first try. It takes superhuman strength not to slam my door closed, but I manage it. No reason to wake up my neighbors because I'm pissed. But I'm not really upset with Hunter. Well, maybe I'm a little upset with him. He should have told me, confidentiality expectations or not. He had plenty of opportunities to say something, and he didn't. But mostly I'm angry at myself.

Only a couple of hours ago, I was making plans to accommodate his presence in my life. I was playing mental gymnastics to figure out how I could start a company and continue to be here with him, more than a thousand miles from my business. Meanwhile, he couldn't be bothered to tell me he might be traded, making all that rearranging unnecessary.

As I wheel my luggage into my bedroom and plop down on the bed, I recognize that I'm being hard on him. Even I know that hockey players don't get much say in the details of their trades, especially young players like Hunter. He wasn't a top draft pick, and he's not one of the biggest names in the league. He'll need to go wherever they send him if he plans to continue playing at the professional level. If I follow that logic, it doesn't matter if I know or don't know he might be traded. The chance is always out there. That's the nature of their job. So though I have a right to be irritated he kept the information from me, there's nothing that my knowing could have changed.

So why do I feel so betrayed?

I replay our entire conversation on New Year's Eve. That would have been the perfect time for him to tell me, but he didn't. Instead, he only said we would make it work wherever we went. That's a pretty obvious message—it says he doesn't want to be part of my life decisions. Didn't I learn anything from my breakup with Nate? I should know that I shouldn't make assumptions about how others feel. Even if they tell me one thing, I should wait to verify the truth.

Ultimately, my frustration doesn't have much to do with him. It has everything to do with me. I'm always willing to bend over backward for everyone, always trying to balance what everyone else wants and what I want. I always want to make everyone happy.

So maybe Hunter is right. Maybe I shouldn't be weighing him into my career decisions. Isn't that what I decided after I broke up with Nate? I told myself I needed to use this time in my life to focus on my goals, and my love life could wait until after that.

Except, that was before I saw how good things could be between Hunter and me. Even considering life without him sends a wave of pain coursing through me. It's not only the physical part. I can't imagine not talking to him every day or not seeing him all the time. He's been the voice of reason in my life for over a year, and I don't want to lose him.

I inhale a deep breath, staring at the ceiling, still wearing my coat. Maybe I should regret my decision to sleep with him, but I don't. Everything about the last month has been amazing.

Rationally, I can't stay at Kellerman. I've already decided that. My remaining questions are all technicalities.

If I take Hunter out of the equation, the most logical thing would be to move to Austin, to be closer to Amanda and Tareek as we get off the ground. But I don't have anywhere to live in Austin unless I want to move back home.

I wrinkle my nose. Living with my parents as I start a company sounds difficult, but it makes the most sense. My dad will understand, but my mother... I predict she won't love the idea of her recent graduate daughter going all in on a risky career. Still, it's logical to live with them. I ran rudimentary numbers last night, and starting the company is expensive. Even with the capital my father and his colleagues plan to invest, we'll need to operate on a shoestring budget.

I glance around at my apartment. It's only the beginning of January. I'll need to look at my lease to find out how long I need to give notice. Usually, it's thirty days, so I would need to pay February's rent. That means I can stay here until the end of next month as we get started and see how things go.

Sighing, I stand and head for the shower. Nothing has changed, technically. Well, except I plan to quit my job in the morning. But neither Hunter nor my situation has changed. He hasn't been traded, and I'm in Philadelphia for at least another month.

Still, everything feels different.

As the water heats, I pull out my phone to make notes for my resignation letter

Hunter

As I head into practice the next morning, I'm already counting the minutes until I can go home and talk to Violet. I texted her first thing, but she didn't answer. At first, I assumed it was because it was early. But as the time she was supposed to be at work passed, my stomach sank. She doesn't want to talk to me.

I didn't sleep well last night, so I'm not in the best mood. When Coach calls me into his office, I smother a flare of irritation. I only want to get in my workout and get out of here today. But I follow him in, and he pulls the door closed behind us.

"You're traded, Mason." He holds his hand out to me. "It's been a pleasure."

Shock vibrates through me as I take his hand. "Traded, sir?" *Not now...*

He nods. "To St. Louis. I believe that's the closest organization to your family."

"Yes, it is." The rink is only a couple of hours from my family's home.

"They want you there tomorrow. The upstairs offices will work with you on travel details. After that, go home and pack your bags."

"Tomorrow." My head spins. That's so fast, but I'm not surprised. Trades happen quickly, expecting acquisitions to hit the ground running in their new building. It wouldn't bother me usually, but things are so wrong with Violet right now...

"Yes." Coach claps me on the shoulder. "Most trades don't bother me. Nature of the business, you know. But I was hoping they would come up with a way to keep you, kid. Like having you in the locker room. Maybe we'll see you again sometime."

"It would be an honor to play for you again, sir," I say, and I mean it. Hargreeves is a fair coach and a good person. I've enjoyed playing for him.

"I wish you the best," he says. Then he winks. "Unless we play you. Then I'll root for you to lose."

My laugh comes out on a bark. "Understandable."

"Now get out of here. And I'll see you around."

At the door, I pause. "Thanks for everything, Coach."

He nods, waving me off.

Dismissed, I head toward my locker. As I stand in front of it, I realize it won't take long for me to pack everything up. I'm as much of a minimalist here as I am at my apartment. Instead of packing, though, I fall heavy on the bench behind me.

Even though I knew I could be traded, the possibility differs from the reality. St. Louis is a dream. I grew up rooting for the team and playing there was my childhood goal. But talk about horrible timing.

"Mason." Duke's voice startles me. The locker room is empty, so he's alone, standing in the middle of the floor in his gear. "Why aren't you dressed, rookie?"

"Traded," I tell him, my voice gruff.

Duke's face falls. "Yeah?" He shakes his head. "Well, damn it. I hoped they'd keep you on."

"Me, too, it seems," I answer.

He saunters over on his skates, doing the awkward walk we all do on the rigid soles. The smack he gives me on the back is jarring. "I wish you the best. That's a great team."

"Thank you."

He studies me. "You don't sound happy."

I sigh. "It's not that. St. Louis is close to home so that part is great. It's just... I think I fucked everything up with Violet."

His brow wrinkles. "How so?"

"I didn't tell her about the trade talks."

"Trades aren't in our control usually."

That's true. Though, someone like him would have a lot more clout in trade talks than I would. He's been the captain here for years, and his contribution to the team and organization is established. But I'm not him. "Yeah, well, Nate brought it up to her last night, when we were all out. Told her I might be involved this week. Made it sound like he knew something." I shrug. "Hell, maybe they mentioned something to him. Who knows?"

"Never liked that guy," Duke offers, leaning against my locker.

"Yeah." I sigh. "But I should have told her first."

He folds his arms over his chest. "I don't know what's going on with you two, or why this might be a big deal. But I know you seem happy together. And I know that this life—the travel, the moves, the rigorous schedule—it's hard on relationships."

"Yeah," I agree. "I don't think it's the hockey life that fucked this up for me. I think I did that all by myself."

"Well, you don't seem like a guy who gives up easily." He pushes off the locker and smacks my shoulder. "In my experience, if a girl takes a chance on you, then it's your job to make sure she never regrets it. So, go. Do whatever you have to do to fix what you screwed up."

When he explains it like that, it sounds so easy. Maybe it is just that easy… and that hard.

"Thanks, Duke. I'll do that." He offers me a superior nod like he just relayed some next-level wisdom. Fucking hockey Gandalf or something. I grin. "Take care, okay? I'll check in when I'm in town."

"You better, or June will beat your ass."

That makes me laugh. June doesn't have a violent bone in her body. She's more likely to send someone to the hospital by overfeeding.

"Later, Mason."

"See you, Duke."

He trundles off toward the ice, leaving me alone to pack up my stuff. Duke could be right. Maybe I've been approaching this wrong. Violet gave me a chance already. She must think there's something worth pursuing between us. Now, I just need to show her we can make it work. Sure, things are going to be harder. I'll be in St. Louis. But I have no problem earning more frequent flyer miles. If it means spending way more time on a plane so I can spend as much time as possible with Violet, that's what I'll do.

Grabbing a duffel, I pack my things quickly and efficiently. I have a girl I need to see.

I go directly to Violet's office from the rink. On the drive, I think through how I want to explain everything to her. But when I get to the front desk and ask for her, the receptionist offers me a tight smile. "Violet Tannehill no longer works her."

I wonder if maybe she's confused. "Violet? She's tall, blonde?"

Her smile fades. "I know who she is. She put in her notice this morning and was released."

Did she quit today? I didn't have time to talk with her yesterday about her meeting in Austin. Apparently, it went well. My stomach sinks, and I rap my knuckles on the desk. "Thank you."

Hurrying outside, I pull up her contact information on my phone. When I drop into her voicemail, I leave a message. "Hey, Vi. I just dropped by your work, and you aren't here. I'm going to come by. Be there in a few minutes."

I refuse to overreact about what this means on my drive. At her door, I hit the intercom. Part of me wonders if she won't let me in. But after a moment, she buzzes me up.

At the top of the stairs, I knock. When she opens the door, the sight of her loosens something in my chest. I exhale a breath I didn't know I was holding. "Violet."

"Hey," she offers, and she's not as enthusiastic. "Come on in."

I want to take her in my arms and hold her. But I don't think she would welcome that right now. Instead, I step around her, and she closes the door behind me. "I stopped by Kellermans first, but they said you don't work there anymore."

She nods. "I gave my notice this morning, and Caitlyn just let me go. Makes sense since I'm not in the middle of a contract. No reason to keep me there."

"So you've gone ahead with the new company." I smile. "Congratulations." Again, I want to hug her, but she's positioned herself across the room, out of reach. Her stance is closed off, so I stay put. "I'm so proud of you."

"Thank you." She braces her hands on the island in the center of the room, and we lapse into uncomfortable silence. It's full of the things I should have said.

Now is as good of a time as any to say them, I suppose. "I'm so sorry, Violet. I should have told you about the trade talks."

"Maybe," she allows. "But I get why you didn't. If there wasn't anything concrete, it was probably stressful to think about moving."

She's right, but it misses the point. "That's not why I didn't tell you, though." I step forward, leaving the island between us, and I wait until she meets my eyes. "I did it because I didn't think you would have given us a shot if you thought I might be leaving. And God, I wanted a chance with you. I found out about the trade talks right after you told Nate we were fake dating, and it felt like my last opportunity to get you to see me."

"So you lied to me?" She glares at me. "Great start to a relationship, Hunt."

I wince because she's not wrong. Still, I try to explain. "I wasn't supposed to say anything, and that was enough at first. But then everything felt so precarious. And as you said, nothing was concrete. Coach even said they would try to keep me here. So I just hoped it would all work out in the end." I walk around the island, toward her, and she allows it. Reaching for her hand, I rub my fingers along her knuckles and stare deep into her eyes. "I feel like it did, too. Being with you has been like winning the lottery. We've always been compatible, but this is even better than I ever expected." Emotion tightens my throat.

She glances away, and I reach for her face, tipping her chin up so she has to look at me when I tell her the most important words I've ever said to anyone. "I love you, Violet. I've loved you for a long time.

And I don't know exactly how this is going to work, but I want to make it work with you. That was all true, and it remains true now." When I cup her cheek in my hand, she closes her eyes, pressing into my palm. Emotion tightens my throat. I inhale, and then I let the other shoe drop. "Because I have been traded now. I found out this morning."

Violet

My eyes find him, and my body stills. "Traded."

He nods. "I found out a few hours ago. To St. Louis Wolves."

The sweet things he said moments ago scatter in my brain. "You might have wanted to lead with that."

He shakes his head. "It wasn't as important."

I step out of his embrace, my head spinning. "Nate was right, then." I cringe at that.

"Seems so." Hunter's mouth thins. "I fly out in a few hours."

"You're leaving tonight?" I've lived within walking distance of Hunter for two years. Now he'll be halfway across the country. When I consider moving to Austin, it's a place I'm familiar with. I've never been to St. Louis. It's like he's moving to a completely blank space.

He nods again. "Yeah. On the red eye. They want me there in the morning. I'm supposed to play for them tomorrow night. My agent is sending me the legal details, but there's talk they want to extend my contract there."

"It's so... fast." I assumed I'd have more time.

"That's how these things work. But it doesn't change what I said. I love you, and I want to be with you, Violet. I've wanted to be with you for so long, I can barely remember a time when that wasn't true. And we can do it. I'm sure we can."

I press my hand to my forehead, forcing myself to breathe. A part of me wants to throw myself into everything he's saying. That we can do this, that we can make a long-distance relationship work between us. Him in St. Louis, and me, shuffling around in Philadelphia and Austin, trying to start a company. But he won't only be in St. Louis. He'll be traveling with the team. The hockey season is long and arduous, and playoffs can run into the summer.

When Nate broke up with me, he said it would be too difficult to see each other like that. I was at college, swathed in a protective cocoon. I'm not that naïve anymore.

"Maybe we can," I allow. Meeting Hunter's pleading eyes, I cock my head. "Make things work, I mean." That's one possibility. But in the past twenty-four hours, I found out he was keeping something important from me, while he was living here, with me. Long distance takes super communication skills. If he could keep a secret like that, we're not off to a great start.

"Maybe we can," he repeats, his brow furrowing.

"We can try, right?" I want to think that love conquers all things, but we've never been apart like this, and that's never been my experience. "Long-distance, I mean."

Now he's glaring at me, and he folds his arms over his chest. "You need to explain what exactly is going through your head right now. Because God knows, I won't understand unless you do."

"We both need to focus on our careers right now." That's the truth I've grasped with both hands since finding out about his trade rumors. I wave at the apartment. "I'm in my lease until the end of February, so I plan to stay here until then while we get the company up off the ground. If I need to fly to Austin, I'll stay with my parents while I work with Amanda and Tareek." I motion to him, and I attempt a smile, even though it feels like stone on my face. "And you'll be getting started in St. Louis. Your parents are close, correct? That's a great place for you. I'm sure they'll be happy to have you nearby." His expression has gone from confusion to anger, so I hurry on. "We'll just see how things go." That sounds so logical. A perfect plan. "This way, even if we can't make our relationship work, we'll still be able to stay friends."

Even considering how it will feel, waiting while our intimacy fades, makes pain squeeze my chest. But I do my best to keep that off my face. The most important thing to me is keeping him in my life, no matter what. We started as friends—best friends. That has to mean something.

He buries his hands in his hair. "You're not listening to me, Vi. I don't want to just 'stay friends.' I told you I love you." He enunciates the three words like that's going to change everything. Like somehow, they're a force field that will keep us from heartbreak.

"I love you, too," I say, waving it off. It's the truth. What started as a friendship is so much more than that now. But that doesn't make anything less difficult. "But I'm only saying that we'll be okay in the end."

"In the end?" He shakes his head. "I don't want an end. I want a beginning with you. I want a forever." His voice shakes, and it's like knives in my chest.

I open my mouth, but the words stop on my lips. He sounds so certain. But I'm not. I swallow. "I think you think that now, but what happens when I don't see you for weeks? Or when we play phone tag for long enough that it gets annoying? What happens when you have new friends I don't know? What happens when I'm working long hours, and I can't sleep and I'm too tired to talk? Or you're jetlagged?" I shrug, feeling helpless. "We'll grow apart, that's what will happen. I'm only saying that staying together this way—" I motion between us, "—is going to be really hard. But we've been friends forever. I know we can hold on to that."

I need to believe that. There can't be anything else.

He steps forward, his movements slow like he's approaching a frightened animal. "Violet Tannehill, I love you." His voice cracks, and I hate the pain on his face. "And what I want from you—what I need—is to know that you love me, too. That you love me enough to give this a real chance. To give us a real chance."

My eyes fill, and I blink hard. His expression storms over. With a quick tug, he pulls me against him. The feel of him surrounding me, cradling me, makes my heart crack open. I feel like I'm bleeding on the inside, but no one else knows. He presses soft kisses to my face, and I can barely breathe. "You're listening, but you need to hear what I'm saying, Violet." His voice is gravelly. "I love you."

I cling to him, and his mouth covers mine. This kiss isn't gentle. It's rough, full of fervor. It's raw and wild, and it threatens to bring me to my knees. He holds me up, his forearms cradling my back as his kiss leaves me panting. I want to stay here, in his arms. I don't want him to leave, to be in St. Louis. The world is better when he's near me.

When he pulls away, he studies my face. With tender fingers, he brushes the hair behind my ears. There's resignation in his eyes. "I love you so much. But we'll need to do this together." He steps back, away from me. My body immediately chills. I want to reach for him, but I don't. "You need to let me know if that's what you want, too."

He squeezes my hand, and then he moves toward the door. When he opens it, the door hinges squeal into the painful silence. "I'll text you when I get there."

He's gone before I can even nod, the sound of his footsteps heavy on the stairs outside. I want to follow him out onto the street. I want to make promises I'm not sure I can keep. Most of all, I want to believe everything he said. But I'm not sure I do.

So all I can do is sink to the floor in the middle of my apartment as tears fall down my cheeks.

Hunter

I DON'T REMEMBER MY walk home. The cold seeps into me, and my fingers are numb when I open my front door, but I don't care.

My sterile apartment greets me. There isn't much here. I should be able to pack most of it in a few boxes. It'll be fast. Almost as fast as Violet gave up on us.

I sink onto the couch and rub my hand over my face.

The ways I could have handled the situation differently flash through my mind. She's right—I should have told her about the trade talks. She shouldn't have heard from Nate. Maybe if I told her how I felt earlier, it would have made a difference as well.

But even as I shift the moving parts of what happened around, I can't help thinking there's more here that I don't get.

She said she loved me back in one breath, but then she immediately counted all the ways we wouldn't work. Violet always struggled with perfectionism. Her worries about failing paralyze her sometimes. I saw it in school, and it was clear when she worried about starting her company. But I never expected her to treat our relationship like that.

It was only a little over a month ago when she told Nate we were dating, and I hoped we could make something real. I figured I could crash and burn because she didn't have feelings for me or because she only saw me as a friend. I never expected she could love me back, but it wouldn't be enough.

Dropping my head in my hands, I want to scream. I want to throw something. Hell, I even want to storm back over to her place, break down the door, and demand we keep talking until I get through to her. But this isn't something I can do for her. I told her how I felt, and if she isn't willing to take a risk and do the work, too, there isn't much I can do to change that.

God, it hurts, though. I thought loving her when she only saw me as a friend was painful. But this? It's different. It's not that she doesn't care about me—it's that she doesn't care enough.

Sitting here feeling bad for myself doesn't change anything. I still need to leave for the airport in five hours. Someone will drive my car to St. Louis, and the Tyrants have a service they use to pack up players who are traded. But I want to get the small stuff together myself. I glance at my watch. They promised to deliver a few boxes by dinner. Right now, I can pack up my suitcases.

I drag my luggage out of the closet. I pull out the clothes I wear the most and pack them up. It should help to distract me, but it doesn't. When the packing boxes arrive, I make quick work of my possessions. It's done faster than I expect, so I'm left with almost an hour to kill before I need to get to the airport. I could just leave and get there early. But there's a small part of me that remains hopeful that Violet will call or show up. That she'll come to her senses.

But she doesn't show up. She doesn't even text. Not when I get in the car service to go to the airport, and not when I wait at the ticket window. By the time I get through security, I accept the truth. All the possibilities we had, the way we've been the past few weeks… it's all over now.

Violet

THE NEXT TWO WEEKS are some weird time warp. Parts of it go faster than they should. I have meeting after Zoom meeting. Some of them are with investors, hashing out the details of our funding, and going over our business plans. There are conversations with banks about additional funding, and there's endless paperwork to fill out.

Most of my meetings are with Amanda and Tareek. I fly into Austin to see the office space they've secured for us. We get the server up and running there, and then we figure out the networking logistics. There shouldn't be any reason that someone needs to be there full-time at first. I'm there for two days, and then I fly back to Philadelphia where my desktop is. We have so much to do with our product before we can show it to any clients.

But when I'm not overwhelmed with work, I barely sleep. Those are the moments that drag, long and painful. It's not my work keeping me awake—it's Hunter.

I miss him. In the quiet moments when I lay down, I want to tell him how it's going. I want to hear his perspective on what we're doing. He's become the voice of reason in my life, and without him, I feel adrift.

We text, but it isn't the same. He gives me small snippets of his days. He tells me he likes the guys in the St. Louis locker room. The team is established, and they're on a winning streak. They're favored in their division, and he's stepped in as a center. I tell him I'm proud of him. We keep things friendly, like before we were a couple. But it's not like it was before. Because he'll tell me he loves me and misses me, and he'll ask when he can see me. Except, our schedules are packed, so I tell him I don't know.

I watch his games every chance I can. I don't know why. Seeing him on the ice hurts, too, but I don't stop. It's like my penance for leaving things like I did with him. I feel like I'm slowly dying without him here.

The company is up and running by the end of January, so I'm ready to move to Austin. I plan to fly out on the first Friday of February because my parents are throwing us a grand opening party the next night. Thanks to lack of sleep, I get my packing done early, so I squeeze in lunch with Penny that day before I fly out.

We meet at a restaurant on the corner near my place, and we barely get our order in before she asks me about Hunter.

I sip my coffee. Seems I survive on coffee and snacks these days. "I think we broke up."

It's true. We still text, but the conversations are getting shorter and less frequent. He begins most of them, and he hasn't messaged me for the past two days.

Her brows drop, and a flush hits her pale cheeks. When redheads get worked up, it's a full-body experience. "What the hell did you do?"

I'm tired, so my nerves are frazzled. "Why do you think it's me?"

She snorts. "Because everyone knows you're the one with the issues."

I glare at her. "If I wanted to be insulted, I would wait and have lunch with my mom in Austin." Penny and I have been friends since we pledged Delta Alpha, and then we were sisters—in the sorority sense of the word. I wonder if having a real sister is like this, all blunt revelations and tough love.

Penny sighs and takes a sip of water. "Oh, honey. I'm not trying to insult you. It's just... this is what I worried about when you told me you and Hunter got together."

"What, that he'd get traded to St. Louis and be a zillion miles away?" I roll my eyes. "If you could tell the future, it would have been nice if you clued me in."

"God, no. I'm dating a hockey player, too, remember? Lots of our friends are dating, engaged, or even married to hockey players. Trades, moves? Part of our life." She points at me. "No, I was worried because you're a huge scaredy cat."

I sit up straighter. "Am not."

"Good comeback, only child." She shakes her head. "Hunter isn't Nate."

"Of course not." I wave her off. "I know that. They're totally different."

She leans in. "Exactly, Violet. Totally different." She falls back in her seat. "Now you're the Nate. Except the real Nate's way more self-absorbed. He didn't feel bad about letting you go. You're too sensitive for that. You're probably beating yourself up."

"I'm not beating myself up," I fire back. She just stares at me, so I lift a shoulder. "Fine, I'm maybe beating myself up a little. But nothing about this is like Nate and me."

"Please. Nate broke up with you because it would be too hard for him to do long-distance. And it sounds like you broke up with Hunter because it would be too hard for you to do long-distance."

The server arrives with our food, so I'm saved from responding. I can only sit there, staring at her. That's not it, is it?

Well, yes, long-distance relationships look hard. I have watched my friends struggle. Constantly missing the person you love takes a toll on a relationship.

But isn't that what I'm already doing—missing Hunter? It's not the missing him that I worried about. It's that I wouldn't be worth missing.

When Nate and I broke up, that's how I felt. He left me behind so easily. Clearly, I wasn't worth missing to him. I ended up missing him and feeling humiliated.

Is that how Hunter feels right now, that he isn't worth being missed? Except, I've told him I miss him. I've told him I love him. I just haven't proven I meant it. But words are empty if you don't back them up. Nate told me he loved me all the time. That was easy enough. It's all the actions that are difficult.

In front of me, Penny scoops a bite of salad into her mouth. Suddenly, I'm nauseous, and I push my bowl of soup away. "I'm Nate."

She pauses, with her fork in her mouth, and looks at me. With a sigh, she sets her fork down and reaches across the table to squeeze my hand. Tears fill my eyes, and I swipe at them, angry.

"You're not Nate, hon. That guy took advantage of you, and you would never do something like that." She leans forward. "You're Violet, with too much armor on. Your default is to take care of everyone else, but you're afraid to let anyone else take care of you.

To rely on someone else." Glancing around, she pats my hand. "Just stuff to think about."

She directs the conversation away after that, but I keep thinking about it. We finish lunch, and I hug her too long outside the restaurant. She squeezes my hands. "Good luck with your business. I know you're going to kill it."

Her simple vote of confidence brings tears to my eyes again. I dab at the corners of them. Stupid lack of sleep is making me super sappy. "You don't know anything about programming, Pen."

She winks at me. "Of course I don't. But I know all about you, Tannehill. When you put your mind to something, you make it happen." Her Uber arrives, and she gives me one more quick hug before sliding into the backseat. I keep waving as she drives off.

I need to hurry to make my flight, so getting myself to the airport consumes my next couple of hours. But as I sit at the gate, waiting for my plane to board, I revisit my conversation with Penny.

Too much armor. A scaredy cat. She's right. I'm afraid of making mistakes. I've always been a perfectionist, so it comes with the territory. Usually, though, I stress about things, overthink, and then I do what needs to be done.

But I didn't do that with Hunter. I just gave up.

My plane boards and takes off, and as we fly into the sunset, I think about how I chickened out.

When we land, I text Hunter. *Can we talk?*

But I don't get a response, not that night or the next morning.

My mother knocks on the door of my bedroom the next afternoon. "Are you ready?"

Standing, I finish putting on my earring. "I think so." I smooth my hands over the black sheath I chose for the Grand Opening party. "How do I look?"

Some mothers might automatically tell their daughters they look beautiful, but my mom isn't like that. She steps in front of me, and she takes in every facet of my outfit. From my low bun to the dangling emeralds in my ears, right down to my pumps. They're satin, with a pointed toe and a slingback. Dressy enough for a cocktail party, but also serious enough for a businesswoman. She studies my makeup, turning me from side to side. Finally, she nods. "You look like an executive if I've ever seen one."

I offer her an apologetic smile. "Not what you expected when you signed me up for all those beauty pageants when I was little, huh?"

I mean it as a joke, but my mother pauses as she reaches for the emerald clutch I left on my bed. It's the slightest hesitation, but I know her. When she straightens, she holds the purse out to me. "No. It isn't. You're much more than I ever expected."

I swallow, accepting the bag, and tucking it under my arm. Under her gaze, I want to squirm, but she taught me better than that. Proper southern women don't squirm.

Just when I expect her to leave it at that, she steps closer. My mother is as tall as I am, and we're both wearing heels, so she looks me right in the eye. She places both hands on my shoulders. "You make me so proud, Violet Jean. Do you know that?"

I'm exhausted, or maybe my emotions are just close to the surface today. After all, Hunter didn't text back, and I have been thinking about how I messed all of that up all day. Either way, my eyes fill with tears as I nod.

Something on my face mustn't be convincing because she narrows her eyes. "I mean it. You're so smart, and I knew from a young age that you would do amazing things. You read early, and you were just like your father. Numbers, calculations, the stock market, all of it. It came so easy for you. Then you started building things. So smart." She shakes her head, grinning. "The world is hard on women, especially smart women. So I wanted to prepare you the best I could. And you were so eager to learn everything, to excel at anything we asked of you." Her smile fades slightly. "I wonder, though, if you worried too much about making us happy, and not enough about making yourself happy."

She pats my cheek before taking my hands in hers. "This work makes you happy. I can tell. And your Hunter, he makes you happy, too." Squeezing my fingers, she smiles, and it might be the most radiant smile I've ever seen on her face. "Your happiness makes me happy."

The tears I've been holding spill out of my eyes. "Hunter…" I can't say anymore, so I glance down and shake my head.

"Oh no," she says. "What happened?"

We sit down on my childhood bed side-by-side. She takes my hand, and the words spill out. I tell her all about how I pushed him away when he wanted to make things work and about how hard the past few weeks have been without him. Crying, I tell her how much I miss him, and how I might be too late.

She listens without a word. When I run out of words, I catch my breath and use tissues to mop up the mess I've made of my face. Finally, she shifts so she can face me. "What do you want, Violet?"

"What?" I don't understand what she's asking me.

"It's not a hard question." She smooths her perfect bangs off her brow. "What do you want?" When I only stare at her, she motions toward my outfit. "You decided you were going to leave your job at Kellermans. A safe job, I might add. A lot of mothers would bring up how safe that was. But not me, of course. You know I love when you take risks." When my startled gaze meets hers, she actually snorts out of a laugh. "You should see your face."

We giggle together, and she wraps an arm around me. "I'm just saying you make your choices and you do what you need to do. Even if they're risky, and even if they stress you out." She cocks her head. "You worry you're going to mess up, but you do it. So what do you want now?"

"This isn't a job, Mom. It's a relationship. It's not as easy as just deciding to do it and then making it happen."

"Well, I think you're wrong. I've been married for a long time." When I tilt my head in question, she laughs. "I mean, you decide every day to do it." She obviously can see I don't understand because she squeezes my hand. "I love your father. But we are very different people. Our marriage is never boring, but it's not always easy. Sometimes it takes work. We both just decide every day to do that work."

She stands, smoothing out her own dress. In pale gray chiffon, she's beautiful. "Now you need to decide what's worth your work. You need to choose if Hunter is worth your work." She studies me, and from the disapproving look she gives me, I'm sure I'm a disaster. "But first, you have a business to launch. And there's no way I'm letting you go to our launch party looking like that." She offers me a hand and helps me up. "Lets get your face put back on. We need to hurry. The party begins at four o'clock."

My mother masterfully tidies my makeup, much faster than I could. In record time, we're heading toward the club. If my father notices anything wrong, he doesn't say so.

On the ride, I think about what my mother said. What do I want? For the past few weeks, I've enjoyed working on the program with Amanda and Tareek. It was the right decision to take this chance. But no matter how happy work makes me, nothing feels right without Hunter.

I want him, and I want to be with him. There are a lot of reasons why our relationship will be hard, but it's hard to miss him too. He's worth a chance. What we have is worth a chance. I can only hope he still feels the same.

Decided, I pull my phone out of the green clutch and search for flights.

Hunter

I SPEND MOST OF the last week of January in bed with the flu. I can't remember being so sick. When my mother catches wind of it, she offers to come with food and supplies. It takes lots of fast talking to keep her at home, but I don't want to get her sick as well. As a compromise, she has groceries and food delivered to me.

By Saturday, I feel better. I head to the rink for fluids and medicine, hoping the training staff will clear me to play that night. We'll be taking on the team from Vancouver, and we need all men on deck. There's lots of debate, but after the team doctors check me out, they clear me to play.

Thank God, too. I score the go-ahead goal in the second period, and we hang onto the lead until the end. We needed the win to stay on top of our division.

But I'm wiped out by the end of the night. It was a late game start to cater to the west coast audience. I take a long shower, and then I drag ass through getting dressed. I don't walk out of the facility until after midnight.

The parking lot is quiet. Light snow flurries fall, highlighted in the lot lights. My Tahoe arrived from Philadelphia last week, and it's parked in the player section. I start it up as soon as my key fob works.

It isn't until I round the driver's side that I see Violet standing next to my truck.

I blink. Maybe I'm feverish again and seeing things. God knows I've thought about her so much over the past few weeks, it wouldn't be a stretch to hallucinate her. She's never far from my thoughts. But she's still there, the closer I get.

"Violet?" I pause a few yards from my car. "What are you doing here?" I haven't seen her since the day I got traded, and I soak her in. Her cheeks are pink from the cold, but as always, she takes my breath away.

I keep a distance between us, though. I have no idea why she's here or what this means. If I get closer, I'll want to reach for her, and I'll probably say stupid things.

"Hi." She steps closer to me. When the light reaches her, I get a better view of her outfit.

"Christ, woman." I hurry forward, dropping my bag on the ground and unzipping my coat. "What the hell are you wearing?"

She's in heels and her legs are bare from the knee down, sticking out from under some kind of black skirt. On top, she's wearing a horrendous sweatshirt with "St. Louis, Missouri" emblazoned on it. She's pulled the sleeves down over her hands, and she's got her arms folded around her body. There's a black scarf wrapped around her neck and up over her head like a hood.

Shrugging out of my coat, I wrap it around her. "How long have you been out here?" I glance around. There are no cars around. "How the hell did you get here?"

I hurry her toward the car door, but when I open it for her, she doesn't get in. Instead, she just stares up at me, a strange smile on her face. "You're here."

"Of course I'm here." I frown down at her. Maybe the cold weather is messing her with heads. If her core temperature has dropped, she could be hallucinating. "I live here. Get in the car before you freeze."

"Hunter," she puts her hand on my arm. "Stop worrying for two seconds, please. I need to talk to you."

The touch of her fingers stops me. My gaze meets hers. She's so gorgeous. Even though I have her face memorized, I'm always struck dumb when I see her. I wonder if that'll always be true. Right now, I just let myself look at her.

The past few weeks have been torture. When I text her, her responses are brief. I kept telling myself I could be patient. But as the days and weeks passed, I lost hope. I could feel us growing apart.

"I love you, Hunter Mason." She cups my face in her hand, and her fingers are freezing, but I don't care. "I love you so much."

"I love you, too, pretty girl." I'm sure I've told her that at least twenty times since I left Philadelphia. Sometimes, I wondered if I shouldn't.

"I know. But I wanted to come here to tell you I want to keep being in love with you." I don't follow, so I shake my head at her. She scrunches up her forehead, and the look—her thinking face—is so familiar it tugs at my heart. "What I mean is, I want to make this work. With you."

"You do?" I need to make sure I don't misunderstand.

She nods. "That's why I came here to see you. So I could tell you that... I was scared. I'm still scared. I just came from the grand opening party for my company, and work is so busy. You're a professional hockey player. We both travel. Everything is still going to be hard. And I don't care. If you still want to make things work with me, I want to make them work with you, and I hope you still feel the same." She squeezes my hand. "I messed up. I'm so sorry. Please. Give me another chance. I should have never let you leave Philadelphia like that. I should have..."

I lean forward and cover her mouth with mine. Her words were getting faster, and when that happens, she works herself up. And right now, she doesn't need to be upset—she needs to be kissing me.

She takes the hint. I pull her against me, and she wraps her arms around my neck. I use this kiss to tell her everything—that I still feel the same, that I can't imagine ever feeling differently.

When she shivers against me, I return to my senses. There's a chance that's the good kind of shiver, the kind that says she wants to get naked. But it's freezing, and she's not wearing nearly enough clothing as it is.

I break our kiss but still hold her against me. "I need to warm you up."

She offers the smallest sound of protest, but I guide her into the passenger seat and close the door behind her. I toss my bag into the backseat before I slide behind the wheel. Good, it's toasty warm in here.

This leads me to the question... "How the hell did you get here?"

She shrugs. "Uber."

When I toss her an incredulous look, she tilts her head. "I bought my plane ticket on my way to the party. It was the eight o'clock flight or I would need to wait until tomorrow." She shakes her head. "I obviously wasn't waiting until tomorrow. So I left the party after a couple of hours and went right to the airport. Then when I got off the plane, I realized I wasn't dressed properly, so I bought this lovely sweatshirt. I don't know your address, so I figured I would try to catch you at the rink. Because by that point, you weren't answering your phone." She waves her hands to punctuate her explanation. "Which, obviously, because you were on the rink. But I couldn't get in that late in the game, so I found your truck and figured I'd wait here."

"In the cold." I scowl at her.

"Well, Andy over there—," she points to the security kiosk, "—he let me stand with him."

"Andy?" I glance in that direction, and sure enough, the security guard waves.

"Yeah." She nods. "Andy."

I turn the lights on. "So you left a party in Austin early, with no coat, and came to St. Louis, where you purchased a tourist sweatshirt and waited in the snowy parking lot for me to finish my game. With—," I point toward the kiosk, "—your new friend, Andy."

"Yes. Exactly. You've got it right." She cocks her head as if she's considering. "But I didn't need a coat in Austin." She points to the scarf still wrapped around her head. "I had my pashmina. I told you before, they're very warm."

I laugh helplessly. "Got it." I lean over, and she meets me over the center console for a kiss. "I love you, Spacey."

"I love you, too, Bossy Man."

Violet

Hunter drives me to his apartment. He sublet with another teammate. "Justin. Nice guy. But I'm looking for my own space."

It's a townhouse on a quiet street. St. Louis isn't a big city, and it's more spread out than Philadelphia.

We're quiet on the way in because Hunter doesn't want to wake Justin. But it didn't matter. When we walk through the door, Justin's in the kitchen with a bowl of cereal. "Hey," he says, his eyebrows raised.

Hunter places his hand on the small of my back. "Justin, this is my Violet. Violet, this is my roommate, Justin Walker." The way he introduces me is adorable, like he's so proud to show me off to his teammate. I must look ridiculous, though, in my dress and cheesy sweatshirt, but Hunter doesn't seem to care. When I meet his gaze, he's beaming.

I step forward, offering Justin my hand. "Nice to meet you."

"Violet, huh?" He shakes my hand. "I've heard a lot about you. You're as lovely as Hunter said."

I nod, but my throat is tight. Even though I hurt him, Hunter didn't seem to give up on me. It's humbling to be loved by him. I never plan to make him regret that.

Justin looks at his bowl. "You know what? I think I'm done with this." He puts the dish in the sink and backs away, toward the hall. "I think I'm just going to get some shut-eye." He points toward the stairs. "I'll see you guys later."

His exit is so fast, if he was a cartoon, there would have been a cloud of smoke behind him. Hunter chuckles. "I definitely think I'll need my own space."

There are so many things I want to discuss with him, including living arrangements, but right now, all I want to do is get into his arms.

Checking to be sure that Justin's door is closed, I step closer, wrapping my arms around Hunter's neck. "Where's your room?"

Apparently, he doesn't need any convincing. Sweeping me up into his arms, he takes off down the hallway next to the kitchen. His room isn't big, but it's signature Hunter—minimalistic and efficient.

Cold medicine covers the night stand. Hunter catches me staring at it. "Flu. This week," he offers. I nod. I guess that explains why we didn't talk. Not that I needed an explanation. I would have understood if he didn't want to keep trying to get through to me. I didn't exactly make it easy for him.

He closes the door behind him, and the heat in his eyes strips me raw. "Hunt, I'm so sorry. I can't tell you enough—"

He lifts his hand, stepping toward me. "You did tell me enough." He pulls me into his arms. "I know you, Violet. I only hoped you would figure it out. I'm glad you did." His faith in me steals my breath. I still don't know what I did to deserve this man, but I plan to spend forever proving to him he'll never need to doubt me again.

He kisses me softly, but it isn't enough. Not right now.

I reach for his sweatshirt, dragging the hem up his body to get my fingers on his warm skin. He gasps against my mouth, and his kiss deepens. When I reach for the waistband of his pants, he growls. The rough sound heats me.

God, I love this man.

What follows is the fastest undressing I've ever done. When Hunter gathers me against him, we tumble together onto the bed in a tangle of limbs. There's nothing sweet or slow about our love-making. I hold on tight, and I hurry him with kisses and touches. When he's got a condom on and he comes inside me, I cry out, tears streaming down my cheeks. He wipes at them with soft fingers. "It's okay, pretty girl. I have you."

I reach for him. I can't seem to get close enough now. "I love you. I love you so much."

We move, sweaty and gasping, panting together. When my orgasm hits, I fly over the edge with him, pressing my fingers into the muscles of his back.

In the aftermath, I try to catch my breath. He smoothes my hair, but it's a lost cause. I can feel bobby pins digging into my scalp, but I'm too tired to do anything about it.

"I'm so glad you're here, Violet," Hunter says, pressing a kiss to my temple.

"I am too." I glance up and smile at him in the moonlight from his window.

"What made you change your mind?" he asks. "I'm not complaining. Hell, I couldn't be happier that you did. I just always wonder how your mind works."

"Penny. And my mother." I trace a circle on his chest where my fingers lay. "I had lunch with Penny yesterday." I cast him a sideways look. "She was not happy that I screwed things up with you."

He tucks his free arm behind his head and scowls. "You didn't screw things up."

I laugh. "Oh, yes, I did." I rub my cheek against him. "I was a scaredy cat. Those were her words."

"She's mean."

"Right?" I continue to slide my fingers along his skin. It's been three weeks since I touched him. I never want to go that long without holding him again. "She said that I was acting like Nate." His growl is pure loyal indignation. I pat him to calm him down. "She said Nate broke up with me because it would be too hard for him to make it work. But she said I broke up with you because I was too afraid to make it work."

We fall into silence for a long moment. "How did that make you feel?" he asks.

I press a kiss to his chest. "She's right. I was afraid. But not of the work. I'm no stranger to hard work." I consider how to explain. "I was afraid that if I trusted you, truly relied on you this way, that I'd only end up heartbroken again." Swallowing, I bite my lip. "But you aren't like him. You're my best friend, the person I can always turn to. I don't know why I didn't realize all of that sooner."

He squeezes me against him and drops a kiss on top of my head. "We got there eventually. What about your mom? I got the feeling she wasn't a fan of me."

I wave that off. "She told me that if you make me happy, that makes her happy." I can almost feel his dubious look. "Seriously. That's what she said."

He only hums. Well, Hunter and my mother will have lots of time to figure each other out. I love them both, so we'll find a way. I continue. "What she said was that I needed to decide what I want."

"Really?"

"Yeah. She basically said that love is a choice every day. That you decide you want to do it, and then you make it happen." That's not exactly how she said it, but that's what I took from our talk.

"Interesting. She's pretty smart."

There are a lot of words I would use to describe my mother. She's beautiful, put together, and disciplined. I always saw my father as the 'smart' one—the one I got my brains from. But that's unfair. My mother isn't like me or my dad, but she's a brilliant social strategist, and she would do anything for the people she loves. I suppose there are lots of ways to be smart.

"So now what?" he asks. "For you. Now what?"

I scowl up at him. "Well, first, you need to stop thinking there are things next for you or for me. From here on, if you want to make this work, there's only going to be 'we.'" His head tilts in question. "I think that's what upset me the most when you got traded. What affects you will affect me too, and vice versa. We need to talk things out."

He salutes. "Aye, aye. I can do that."

"Okay." I nod against him. "So, I guess we need to decide what's next for us."

"Well, how's your business going in Austin?"

"It's great. The office is small. Amanda goes in, because she's the one who needs to be there. She does most of the hardware portions. But Tareek and I can work remotely. At least for now."

"If that's true, how would you feel about working remotely from St. Louis?" He motions around us. "It's a nice city. Not as big as Philadelphia—which I prefer—but big enough, I think. It's got an airport, so we can fly wherever you need. How long did it take you to get here tonight?"

"Two hours."

"That's not too bad, right? It's a long day trip, but it's doable, if you really needed to."

"Are you asking me to move in with you, Hunter Mason?" I ask teasingly.

"I am asking you to move in with me, to be with me forever. To go where I go, or asking you if I can go where you go. I figure we'll work out the details." He pauses, meeting my eyes. "We."

My eyes fill. When I boarded the plane earlier, I hoped I wasn't too late for us. I assumed I would have some explaining to do. But he's right here, willing to give me a chance again.

Like he really does love me.

"Then, yes. To all of that. Yes to 'we' forever."

Epilogue

Violet

HUNTER AND I MOVE into our rancher at the beginning of March. We opted to rent for six months and see how things went with the Wolves and my company. Having our own space is a gift. Hunter had already agreed to sublet February with Justin, and I didn't want to intrude on them. I spent the short month flying between Austin, St. Louis to see Hunter, and Philadelphia, where I closed up my apartment and put the rest of my things in storage.

The Wolves are out of town for moving day, so my mother flew in from Austin to help. Thank God. No one knows how to direct traffic like Mom. If she hadn't devoted her life to volunteering and taking care of my father and me, she would have made a stellar CEO.

By the time she leaves on the third, I'm exhausted. I don't sleep much, but my mother might be a vampire. I manage a shower, though. I spent the morning painting our bedroom, so I'm a mess. After that, all I have the energy for is to order a pizza and open a bottle of wine.

I must have dozed off on our new couch, though, because the sound of the doorknob turning wakes me. Hunter steps in, dropping his overnight bag at the door.

I spring off the couch and rush into his arms. He's only been gone for a few days, but after our previous hiatus, I hate being apart.

He catches me against him, and I wrap my legs around his waist, pulling him close. Holding me easily with one arm, he closes the door behind him. In between kisses, he gets out, "You didn't lock the door."

"Safe. Neighborhood," I say, punctuating each word with a kiss.

He leans his head back to scowl at me. "No way, Spacey. If I'm not here with you, that door needs to be locked."

"Have I ever told you how much I love it when you boss me around?"

He glares, but when I pull his mouth toward mine, he gives in, giving me the real kiss I want.

"I missed you," I breathe out between kisses.

"Me too, pretty girl."

The doorbell rings, interrupting us, and he lets me slide down the length of his body. He waits until I plant my feet on the floor and I'm steady before he lets me go. "What's that?"

"I ordered pizza."

"You're a domestic goddess."

"I am, aren't I?" I grin at him, opening the door.

I sign for our dinner. When I'm back inside, I hold out the pizza to him. "You have a serious decision to make, Mason."

His brows lift. "I do?"

I nod solemnly. "Pizza—," I hold up the box, "—or sexy times." I use my spare hand to wave down the length of me.

His eyes drag from the tips of my bare toes, up over my sweats and hoodie, right to the top of my still wet hair. The heat that lights his gaze warms my stomach. "No contest."

He doesn't give me any warning when he swoops forward and lifts me up, pizza and all. I squeal, laughing. We pause in our miniscule kitchen for me to drop the pizza on the counter before he carries me into the bedroom.

When we get there, he pauses. "You painted."

"I did," I tell him. "What do you think? My mother helped me pick the color." We chose a sage green. It complements the comforter set I ordered last week.

He sets me on my feet, but he doesn't allow me to get far. Instead, he wraps his arm around my shoulder, drawing me into his side. He drops a kiss on my head. "You did a great job. Thank you."

"I mean about the color, Hunt. What do you think?"

He shifts so he can hold me in the circle of his arms. When I meet his gaze, his expression is full of wonder and love. "It looks wonderful. But you could have painted this room fluorescent colors, polka dots, whatever, and I don't care, as long as you promise to share it with me." He leans down and drops the sweetest kiss on my lips.

I lean into him, as always. "I love you, Hunter. And I'll go where you go. We'll go together."

"Yes, we will," he agrees. "We. For always."

About the Author

Josie Blake writes contemporary romance with sass and emotion. Originally from a small town in western Pennsylvania, she now battles traffic in southern New Jersey where she lives with her hero husband and their happily-ever-after: two very energetic sons. When she isn't writing, she can be found next to a hockey rink or swimming pool, cooking up something sweet, or hiding from encroaching dust bunnies with a book. She loves to hear from readers so please feel free to drop her a note or visit her website at josieblake.com. Connect with her on Instagram at instagram.com/josieblakeauthor, or on Facebook at Facebook.com/JosieBlakeAuthor

Made in the USA
Las Vegas, NV
26 March 2026